Phyllis

A Detroit Heroine

RAYMOND O'SLATTERY

The story of a remarkable woman who symbolizes the unsung mothers of the world, the story of the city of Detroit, the story of a marvelous new school opened just before the Great Depression, and the story of an American family.

iUniverse, Inc.
New York   Bloomington

Phyllis
A Detroit Heroine

iUniverse books may be ordered through booksellers or by contacting:

iUniverse
1663 Liberty Drive
Bloomington, IN 47403
www.iuniverse.com
1-800-Authors (1-800-288-4677)

ISBN: 978-1-4401-7440-7 (sc)
ISBN: 978-1-4401-7442-1 (dj)
ISBN: 978-1-4401-7441-4 (ebk)

Printed in the United States of America

iUniverse rev. date: 09/30/2009

Thanks to:

Ann Marie Sabath

Dedicated to:

My children and grandchildren, my brother,
nephews Matt and Dan, and Sue

Author's Note

"Despite being only four feet eleven inches, she
was always the tallest person in the room."

This is the story of a remarkable woman, the story of an American family, the story of the beginning of a new high school that served as a sanctuary for a group of Depression era students, and the story of the once great city of Detroit. Finally, it is the story of all the unsung mothers in the world.

Phyllis Katherine Arquette was born on October 27, 1916. She was the fifth child born to William Arquette and Hanna Stockdale. She died one month short of her ninetieth birthday. Phyllis Arquette would be called "gifted" today. She possessed remarkable social, political, leadership, and organizational skills. Had she been born fifty years later, Phyllis, who was my mother, might have run for governor, senator, or some other high political position. She achieved remarkable success considering the "hand she was dealt."

Phyllis Arquette's most remarkable success was to raise or help raise three families. When Phyllis was eleven her mother died, and she was to become the protector and surrogate mother for her two younger siblings. She married William O'Slattery, himself a gifted and remarkable person, and they raised their three children. Their daughter, Nancee, died in an automobile accident when she was thirty-two years

old. Nancee had two young boys at the time. They were both in the car
when their mother died. Phyllis ultimately played a major part in the
raising of these two boys.

Phyllis was the first female senior class president in her high
school's history, and one of the first women to receive a scholarship
to the City College of Detroit (now Wayne State University). Her
husband died at the age of sixty-three, and Phyllis lived the last
twenty-six years of her life as a single lady. But she kept active and
became involved in clubs and other activities. She was the president
of the Garden Club of Northville, Michigan; and then the president
of the Garden Club of Michigan; and then the national president of
the Garden Club. She ran most of the things she became involved
with. After the deaths of her husband and her daughter, she vowed
to not give up on life. She wrote and placed on her refrigerator the
following: "Keep moving Phyllis, always keep moving." People would
sometimes say that "despite being only four feet eleven inches, she was
always the tallest person in the room." In her high school yearbook
one of her teachers wrote, "She is little but she makes herself heard."
She was an extremely complex woman, as I hope you will discover in
this book.

Phyllis is also a story of the "love of her life," her husband, William
(Bill) O'Slattery. Besides being a great student, Bill also was a class
president and a remarkable athlete. He was the first person at Mackenzie
High School to be named to the All-City and All-State football teams.
He went on to play college football. He became an automotive engineer
and had a very successful career at the Ford Motor Company

This book also is meant to be a story of the city of Detroit,
Michigan. Detroit was a fantastic place to live. When Phyllis and Bill
were growing up, Detroit was a city that had a great blend of the French
culture and the new American culture. There were many educational
activities in Detroit and fun things to do. It was a safe city in which
children could play outside and move freely around this metropolis
without fear. Children as young as eight or nine could take buses and

streetcars throughout the city. The streetcars traveled from the Detroit River all the way to Eight Mile Road. Detroit named some of its city streets by the miles they stretched from the Detroit River.

Had certain events not occurred and certain attitudes not developed, Detroit would have become one of the greatest cities in North America. There is still a tremendous amount of "brainpower" in and around Detroit. The automobile industry and other industries made it a manufacturing giant. It is a "sleeping giant" that could wake up soon. Its nickname became the "Motor City." There are many major universities in the area that are still ready to revitalize Detroit. Detroit had one of the first expressway systems. It recognized early the importance of parks and culture. The Fox Theater and the Detroit Institute of Arts are examples of the culture. Magnificent parks are still at Belle Isle, Palmer Park, and Rouge Park. Detroit has embraced its dance halls, symphonies, artists, singers, and writers. It truly could still be "The Paris of the Midwest," as it was once called.

I include the glory days of Detroit because my parents and their families loved it so much. It is sad that it has such a bad reputation today. There are many causes of this, and it is not the purpose of this book to analyze them. What I do want to say is that I am optimistic that the city can regain its glory. Detroit has great people. There are signs that a renaissance is about to happen. The new sports fields and the renovation of the Fox Theater are examples of this trend.

Detroit was part of the "arsenal of democracy" in both World War I and World War II. The dedication, organization, and abilities of the people in Detroit helped win two world wars. Men and women by the thousands volunteered to fight in these wars. Bobbie Arquette, the brother of Phyllis, was a decorated soldier who fought in the Battle of the Bulge. Oliver Karson, the best man at the O'Slatterys' wedding, fought across Europe in helping to defeat fascism.

Detroit has always loved its sports and sports heroes. Detroiters are extremely loyal to all of their teams. Joe Louis adopted Detroit as his hometown. Ty Cobb and Hank Greenberg were early baseball heroes.

Greenberg was one of the first Jewish baseball stars. Gordie Howe has been called "Mr. Hockey" and is considered one of the all-time greats. Bobby Layne led the Detroit Lions to National Football League championships in the 1950s. Detroit has always loved the Red Wings, the Tigers, the Lions, and the Pistons (after they moved to Detroit from Fort Wayne, Indiana, in the 1950s). Detroiters have supported their teams, win or lose.

I hope the reader discovers a remarkably romantic city; and the reader will find it was a slightly naïve time despite the bad economic times of the 1930s. I have included some of the things written in school newspapers. They show an innocence that permeated the American society at that time. I have included information from articles written in Detroit newspapers and other sources. They show a magical history.

As I revised the book and read and reread my parents' scrapbooks, and the more I remembered about my childhood, I came to realize how important Mackenzie High School was in their lives. I wondered how they could be so "caught" in the past. But I realized that this new Mackenzie High School became their second family. It was much bigger than "just" a school for my parents and the other classmates described in this book. Sadly, it closed in 2007 (one year after my mother passed away).

This book is fiction based on fact. Some of the episodes described are exaggerated. The stories of Johnny O' Slattery and my grandfather's involvement with Irish Jimmy Slattery were put together by a few stories my grandfather told me. He would say they were his cousins. But I don't think they were. He told me about the Purple Gang and bootlegging one day after I played in a Little League play-off game. He talked about a cousin of his that was involved in bootlegging. He came to this game by himself and it was very special to me. We lost the game, and our long conversation afterward soothed the hurt of the loss. It was the longest conversation I ever had with him. The stories of Jimmy Slattery were from conversations he had with our family during our dinners together. I am not sure if they were Irish blarney or the truth.

My father did tell me that Grandpa O'Slattery followed the career of his "cousin" and sometimes went to his fights. I included the stories of Johnny O'Slattery and Irish Jimmy Slattery to show the history of the times. But the stories of my parents' successes are not exaggerated.

The stories of Raymond O'Slattery's drinking are from innuendos I heard as a child. The subject was rarely talked about. If my father had a few extra drinks, my mother would always say, "You are becoming just like your father." This stopped my father in his tracks. Therefore, the stories are symbolic of "bits and pieces" that I heard. I wish to emphasize that my grandfather was a distinguished and good man.

This book will mainly follow the early life of Phyllis Arquette. It will more briefly describe her own family and then how she helped raised her daughter's young boys. Phyllis lived several lifetimes in one. She was a lady with a great wit, sometimes biting. She was a lady who was free with compliments and made people feel good. She never met a waitress that was not the best waitress that had ever served her. She seemed to wear down in later life. She developed Alzheimer's disease in her eighties and sadly deteriorated in her last several years. I hope the reader will discover a remarkable person and agree with me that my mother was truly one of the unsung mothers of the world. I hope this book can be an inspiration to others. They will discover a strong person who once said, "I am flexible as long as I get my own way."

Early History Of Detroit

I think it is important to look at a short history of Michigan and specifically Detroit. The reader is free to skip this discussion at this point and go directly to Part 1, Chapter 1. But I do recommend that at some point the reader return to the early history. I have saved many of my lesson plans from my teaching years. The following is from a lesson plan I prepared while I was student teaching in Northville, Michigan. The sources are not known to me anymore. I got the information from the Cooke Middle School library and the library at Eastern Michigan University.

The land that would become Michigan was once covered by glaciers. The glaciers moved north approximately fifteen thousand years ago. What remained was fertile land, thousands of acres of timber, thousands of varieties of animals and plants, and of course, the magnificent Great Lakes. As most people know, Michigan is divided into two parts—the Upper and Lower Peninsulas. Together they look like a large rabbit jumping over a large mitten. People in the Lower Peninsula like to use their hand in the shape of a mitten and point out where they are from. Detroit is "right below the thumb," people from Detroit like to say. Native Detroiters place the accent on the second syllable, whereas many around the country like to say Détroit, with the accent on the first syllable. This is tremendously annoying to many Detroiters.

Detroit is midway between Lake St. Clair and Lake Erie. It is along what is called the Detroit River. Technically, it is not a river but a strait—a body of water connecting two rivers or seas. The name "Detroit" means "strait" in French. Detroit was built along an extremely flat plane—the highest point in the entire city being a mere 110 feet above sea level. The area was originally inhabited by Native American tribes—mainly the Chippewa, the Wyandot, and the Huron. French trappers and explorers were the first Europeans to sight this area. One can actually stand on the shore of the Detroit River and look south and see Canada, as a finger of Canada juts out south of Detroit. Its climate can be harsh—the Great Lakes influence the weather and can make it change in a hurry. "If you don't like the weather, wait a few minutes," is an ongoing joke in Detroit. Its prevailing westerly winds, however, have suited its manufacturing culture well, as pollution is relatively low for such a large city.

Antoine de la Mothe Cadillac is given credit for being the founder of Detroit in 1701. He convinced Louis XIV to build a fort to protect the fur trade. The Indians and the French got along fairly well, but when the British/Yankees started moving west, hostility began between the European American culture and the Native American culture. The Indians mostly sided with the French in the "French and Indian War" ("Seven Years' War," as it is called in Europe), but the British were able to capture the fort in 1760. Still the area was mostly settled by the French up until the mid-1850s.

The Indians did not like the British very much and were often rebellious. The most famous uprising was led by Chief Pontiac and became known as the "Pontiac Conspiracy (1763-1765)." There was not much action around Detroit or other parts of this territory during the Revolutionary War.

Detroit was officially incorporated in 1805. However, a few years later it almost disappeared as a viable city when a huge fire started in the stable of John Harvey and destroyed most of the town. But the resiliency of the people was evidenced by the fact that the entire city was rebuilt by 1825. New Englanders started moving to Detroit at about this time. Its culture was still predominately French, and it was starting to get the reputation of being the "Paris of the West.". There were two thousand inhabitants living in Detroit in 1830; however, by 1855 there were thirty thousand. One immigrant Irishman at this time was John Ford, whose grandson was Henry Ford.

Two events led to the growth of Detroit. The first was the completion of the Erie Canal. Through this canal and the Great Lakes, the East could meet the West. The other event was the discovery of copper and iron ore in northern Michigan. These led to the metamorphosis of Detroit into a manufacturing city. The first nickname of Detroit was the "potbelly stove capital of the world." Soon, Detroiters began producing railway equipment, boats, and marine engines. These skilled workers would someday be available to help Detroit become "king" of the automobile industry.

Detroit soon became an ethnic melting pot. The Irish, Germans, Poles and other Eastern Europeans, and, of course, the French were the primary European groups. There was still a population of Native Americans, but many of those still remaining in Detroit had mixed with the French. Some say that nearly everyone with a French surname living in or near Detroit is partly Native American, even though this is difficult to corroborate. African Americans also began to migrate to Detroit. Bad times in agriculture and the attraction of jobs in Detroit led to this migration.

Detroit grew outwardly toward the west rather than the north. There were few apartment complexes. As the city grew, it simply built more single-family dwellings and duplexes. This was one of the country's first urban/suburban sprawls. In fact, two cities in the middle of the geographic region of Detroit—Hamtramck and Highland Park—were simply encircled. They became "islands" surrounded by Detroit. By the 1920s, there were approximately one million people in Detroit.

It was mainly the automobile industry that made Detroit grow, and it was this industry that shaped the character, culture, and psyche of the city. In 1910 there were thirty-eight automobile companies in Detroit, and by 1917 they were producing over one million automobiles a year.

By the mid-1920s, the city of Detroit was dominated by the genius of Henry Ford. Henry was born in 1863 near Dearborn, a city next to Detroit. At an early age, he was fascinated by the machinations of watches and clocks. As a teenager, he began earning money by repairing them. He was showing early signs of the entrepreneurship that would follow. He quickly learned to be a mechanic and was hired as an apprentice. He worked as an apprentice until the age of twenty-two, mainly working on steam engines and farm machinery. In 1884 his father purchased a farm for him, but he was not suited for this type of work. After two years, he returned to Detroit and obtained a job as an engineer for the Detroit Edison Company. Behind his home in a shed, he began to work on his first automobile. He studied the designs of European car manufacturers such as Benz. He completed his first car in the late 1890s using the internal combustion engine. He used an electric bell for a horn and a steering lever rather than a steering wheel. It had only four horsepower, but it was the beginning of much bigger things to come.

In 1899 he helped to organize the Detroit Automobile Company. Initially, car manufacturers made cars by order, so their cost made them unaffordable to most. In 1903 Ford founded the Ford Motor Company. He raised $28,000 in cash to start his company. One of the initial $2,000 investors made $5 million in dividends by 1919. He eventually sold his stock in the 1930s for $30 million, a massive fortune at that time.

Ford was a visionary. His idea was to make interchangeable parts and to mass-produce affordable, high-quality automobiles. He invented the assembly line to produce his products. He initiated the $5.00 workday so that his workers could afford his Motel T's. He also wanted to produce cars from the raw materials to the final product. To do this he made steel factories, railroads, and steamship lines. The Rouge complex was the end result of this.

When our story starts in 1928, Bill O'Slattery is thirteen and knows he wants to work for this majestic industry someday.

Part I

Chapter 1

"She may be little, but she makes herself heard."

It is a hot, humid summer day in Detroit, Michigan. It is a day on which a great romance will start. There is a small island in the Detroit River called Belle Isle. It is one of the favorite places for Detroiters to go for amusement. On this day, the island is crowded with adults and children. Phyllis Arquette is playing field hockey with several of her friends. Bill O'Slattery is playing a game of tackle football with his friends.

In the summer of 1928 Detroit is an exciting place to live. Manufacturing is king for sure. But Detroit is about much more. Culture, the arts, sports, entertainment, education, and romance are all blooming. It is the Roaring Twenties and Detroit is roaring like no other city. Flappers, blind pigs, bathtub gin, speakeasies, and bootleggers are becoming commonplace in Detroit. Ty Cobb is now playing for the Philadelphia Athletics, but his memory and soul will always be in Briggs Stadium, the fantastic baseball field of the Detroit Tigers. Baseball is supreme, especially when the hated Yankees and Babe Ruth are in town. Babe Ruth hit sixty home runs the last year. Win or lose, Detroit loves its sports teams. Usually, when people think of Detroit in 1928, they think of cars, Henry Ford, the Model T, assembly lines, and factories. However, the essence of Detroit was its readily available amusements and romanticism. Young and old could visit Belle Isle, Bob-Lo Island, or the Graystone Ball Room, take a trip downtown on the streetcar, visit the Vernors Factory to have a Boston cooler or a "brown cow" soda, enjoy Sanders candy or hot fudge, visit one of the many ice cream parlors, sit at the soda fountain at a dime store, visit the Fox Theatre, or visit the exciting Detroit waterfront.

The epitome of Detroit's romantic soul is Belle Isle. It is where Phyllis Arquette and Bill O'Slattery will first meet and later have some of their most wonderful moments. It is great time to be growing up in the Motor City.

Belle Isle is green and vibrant on this summer day of 1928. It is exciting like the city. However, it goes much further because of its romantic, idealistic appeal. On one of the green athletic fields is a group of young girls who are playing field hockey. The girls are between the ages of ten and twelve. On another field is a group of boys about the same age. They are playing tackle football without pads. Nearby are groups of children sunbathing and swimming at the small, pristine beach. Their noise can be heard throughout the island.

Belle Isle has an interesting history. It is located about a half mile from old Fort Detroit, the site of what is now downtown Detroit. It is long and thin and about one-half mile in length. The southern tip resembles the shape of an arrowhead. It was originally called Wahnabezee (Swan Island) by the Native American tribes who inhabited the area when the French first explored the Great Lakes. Its primary tribes were the Ottawa and Chippewa, who hunted on the island and made temporary shelters. The French were the first Europeans to enjoy its natural beauties.

With the ascendancy of the English in North America, the French gradually lost interest in the island. And, of course, the Native Americans were not consulted when King George granted a Lord McDougall ownership of the island and changed the name to Hog Island. Lord McDougall paid 194 pounds sterling—a bargain even for that time. The first survey indicated that it measured 704 acres. When Ty Cobb was traded to the Athletics, it had grown to almost 1,000 acres through the rise and fall of the river.

Lord McDougall did not hold the island for long. With the Treaty of Paris after the Revolutionary War, Hog Island became a territorial possession of the new United States of America. Lord McDougall still had title to the property, but he sold it in 1794 to William Macomb for 813 pounds. There is a county named after Macomb near present-day Detroit. The Macomb family sold it to Barnabas Campau for $5,000 in 1817. The first ferry boat service started in 1840 and the name was changed to Belle Island in 1851, as the new owners thought the old name was not fitting for such a beautiful place.

The city of Detroit acquired the island in 1879. Detroit wanted a park that would emulate the parks and tree-lined boulevards of Paris. The French influence was still very prevalent in Detroit. In 1883, the city hired Frederick Law Olmsted to build a masterpiece. He is famous for designing Central Park in New York City, as well as parks in Chicago, San Francisco, and Boston. In order to make Belle Island a park for heavy structures, the designers decided to build ditches for drainage and to fill in the marshes. These marshes were dredged to create canals, small lakes, and lagoons. The fill was used to build up the adjacent areas, which ultimately became grassy fields. Originally it was covered by forests. Olmsted insisted that some of these be preserved. By the 1920s there were still two hundred acres of forest. Deer were stocked on the island and ran wild. Over time, the name was shortened from Belle Island to Belle Isle.

Belle Isle possesses dozens of different trees, plants, and other flora. It is a natural migratory flyway for waterfowl. By the late 1920s, the island was home for a conservatory, an aquarium, a casino, a yacht and boat club, a band shell with a dancing floor, an athletic shelter, a picnic pavilion, a "white" house for the superintendent, maintenance and repair quarters, riding stables, numerous bridges, and a "love canal." Olmsted and Detroiters felt that "this park has the power to divert men from unwholesome, vicious and destructive behavior by providing recreation and self-education opportunities."

The field hockey game is spirited. The athletic pavilion on the island issued field hockey sticks and a ball. It is just a pickup game; the girls follow their own rules. Most of the four girls on each side charge to the ball as if in a swarm of bees. One side is slightly more organized. An extremely slight girl with blonde curly hair frantically moves a few feet from the ball—thin legs moving so fast they can hardly be seen. She constantly yells out orders to the rest of the teammates. "Get the ball," "play your position," "pass," "stay low"—constant orders. Oddly enough, the other girls, although much bigger, enthusiastically try to do what she orders. She is eleven years old, just over four feet tall, weighing sixty pounds at the most. Her ability, except for her speed, is not good, but her loud, high voice makes up for her size.

The boys playing tackle football grunt and howl. Their grass-stained trousers and shirts are wet with sweat and mud. There are no uniforms for this group. In the 1920s, football is almost all running plays. It is more like rugby with lots of laterals. There are four players on one side and five on the other. One boy, age twelve, is dominating. Close to six feet tall and about 165 pounds, he is much bigger than the other boys. He is always chosen to be on the side with the lesser numbers because he is so rough and dominating. On offense he is the center, never choosing to carry the ball or pass. He blocks two or three of the other players on each offensive play. He is like a one-person "flying wedge." On defense he always chooses to stand slightly behind the line of scrimmage. He roams sideline to sideline, always following the ball. It is as if the ball and he are magnetic. He makes almost every tackle and every play. Rarely talking, he lets his actions speak for him.

There is a small beach on Belle Isle, and because of the ninety-degree August heat and the humidity of Detroit, it is completely covered with joyous boys and girls. Most of them are under ten years of age; however, a few older girls lie on blankets basking in the sun. It is the Roaring Twenties, so girls' bathing suits are starting to get skimpier. Inside the women's bathhouse, there is still the sign that was placed in 1908. It reads:

White & Flesh Colored Suits prohibited,
Or suits that Exposes Chest lower than a line,
Drawn on a Level with the Arm Pit,
Suits must have skirts not shorter,
Than Four inches Above the Knee and,
Bottom of Skirt must not be Shorter than,
Two inches above bottom of Trunks,
Arm Pits must be covered.
Dept. of P & R

But times have changed. Young ladies are no longer following these rules. They are wearing lipstick and makeup. The smell of cigarette smoke is now common in the bathhouse.

Two of the twelve-year-old girls sit separately from the smaller children. One of these girls is a tall, blonde German American young lady. Starting to mature, she is not too bashful to show much more of her body than ordinarily would have been permitted in 1928. She is a beautiful young lady—a natural beauty with long, blonde hair and glowing, slightly tanned skin. When they're not being seen, teenage lifeguards constantly look her way.

It is close to seven o'clock and the last ferry to Detroit is about to leave. The games stop, the swimmers return to the bathhouses, and the kids start to return to the dock. The petite, curly-haired blonde girl is close to the front of the line. She is with her older sister, Doris. In front of them is the blonde girl admired by the lifeguards. The line quickly gets longer. Soon the football players arrive. They are loud and boisterous as they try to get the attention of the girls. The largest boy walks slowly to the front of the line, trying to get the attention of Natalie, the girl from the beach.

"Hey, Natalie, how are you doing?" he asks in a voice that has already changed from that of a boy to that of a man.

"Great, Bill. What about you?" she replies flirtingly.

Before he could answer, the little girl with the blonde curls yells out, "Hey, buster, no cutting in line. Who do you think you are?"

Startled and embarrassed, Bill quietly says he is sorry and returns to the end of the line with his buddies. Phyllis and Bill have met.

In the background is the skyline of Detroit. The newly completed skyscrapers called the Penobscot Building and the Fisher Building can be seen. The city looks new and exciting. The Ambassador Bridge can also be seen. It was finished in 1920 and is now the largest suspension bridge in the world. It will become the conduit for the busiest international crossing in North America. It is an engineering marvel that symbolizes the ingenuity of the people of Detroit.

Bill O'Slattery, the football player, now at the end of the line, looks back at the beautiful green Belle Isle. He loves going there. He is very serious and very confident and knows that good things are going to happen to him. He knows this despite his tumultuous home life. Physically and mentally mature beyond his age, he has an inner confidence that makes him feel he is destined for success. He feels the vitality of the city inside him. All socioeconomic classes feel they can achieve. After all, this is the town of Henry Ford and the Motel T.

Bill loves coming to Belle Isle because it is an escape from his home life. He is the son of two intelligent Irish American parents, whose ancestry traces back to Ireland. He loves the beauty of Belle Isle and has studied its history. He has hiked and canoed through its woods, canals, lagoons, small lakes, and fields. He could be a tour guide. Now he embarks on the ferry and patiently awaits the ride back to Detroit.

The ferry begins to fill up as seven o'clock approaches. The chatter is infrequent because the children are tired and sad to leave. The ferry leaves the island and arrives at the docks at Grand Boulevard at 7:20 PM. The young, spunky blonde girl and her sister quickly disembark and hurry to the streetcar that will take them to their home. They can get off the streetcar near the intersection of West Chicago Street and Wyoming Avenue, which is close to their home. They love taking the marvelous streetcars. When they get off the streetcar, they run on the railroad tracks that are attached to the electrical lines that power the cars. These streetcars transport workers, shoppers, and children back to their homes. Crime is low and the city is very protective of its younger people.

Phyllis and her sister Doris arrive at their home around 8:00 PM. There is no daylight saving time, so the sun is quickly setting. It is a bright red, purple, pink, orange sunset—a "sailor's delight," as they are fond of saying in Michigan.

Chapter 2

D inner is never early at the Arquette home. William Arquette works from dawn to dusk on most days, Monday through Saturday. He is a mechanic in a local shop. He possesses only a tenth-grade education, yet is remarkably talented with his hands. He works on most of the engines in the burgeoning technological age. Fixing cars, especially the Model T, has become his specialty. The Model T is a fantastic automobile. It has extremely thick metal on the outside, which makes it almost impossible to dent. Detroiters of the 1920s loved to drive their new automobiles on the "open road." An "open road" in 1928 meant no road at all. It has been called the first "SUV." The constant hammering from holes in the fields and from streets which were mostly made of brick caused a demand for mechanics. William Arquette had lots of work. But it was not just the Model T that needed repairs. There were still over thirty automobile companies in Detroit in 1928. William also had plenty of work repairing farm machinery. Even though they lived in the middle of Detroit, the Arquette family was not far from the farmlands of southeastern Michigan. America was still mainly a rural/farming country.

William Arquette loved to work. He loved getting his hands dirty from the grease and grime of the machines because it made him feel useful and important. The work ethic was the major value and driving force in Detroit at this time. Wages are getting better and better. Henry Ford introduced the five-dollar day for his automobile workers, and this spread to most of the other business. A few businesses were unionized, but the unions were not as needed as they would be later. William had a thin face. He was of average height and was extremely thin. His hair was thinning and his face was leathery from his early days working on a farm. He had a gaunt look to him. When he smiled, creases readily appeared in his cheeks. He moved from the countryside to Detroit in 1910 when his family farm failed. He was part of an urbanization trend. Never looking back, he relished the idea of the big city and the endless opportunities of the age of manufacturing in southeast Michigan.

Dinner was ready at half past eight—the normal dinner hour for the Arquettes. Like most wives and mothers in 1928, Hanna Arquette accepted her role in the family. The father/husband was supposed to be the "breadwinner," and the mother/wife was supposed to raise the children and run the home. William and Hanna Arquette had seven children—above average for the times but not unusual. Hanna was a petite woman, who looked much younger than her forty-two years of age. She wore her hair up because she liked to show her pretty, delicate face. She liked it when people called her pretty and liked it when they said she sure did not look like a woman who had given birth to seven children. She was part Irish, German, French, and Native American. She had green eyes with a rosy complexion. She always bragged that she did not need the makeup being worn by the modern woman of the 1920s. Her height was less than five feet and she weighed less than one hundred pounds.

Donald was the oldest of the seven children. He was twenty-five years old. He was born when Hanna was seventeen years old. He had moved out of the house when he was in his late teens and was now married. Standing five foot three and weighing only 120 pounds, Donald always felt robbed by this small stature. He was extremely self-conscious about his height and hated to be kidded. Calling him "shorty" was a bad idea, because he was tough and ready for a good fight.

Marvin, the next oldest at twenty-one, had recently moved out of the house, but was home today to take advantage of another marvelous meal prepared by the mother he adored. Marvin was also short, about five foot six, but he was much stouter than his brother Donald. He had a "happy-go-lucky" personality and was the type of person everyone liked. People would be hard pressed to ever remember when he was not in a good mood. He was always eager and willing to help others.

Marvin was sitting in the parlor reading *The Detroit News* when a loud automobile horn screamed out. This must be sister Tulah, he instantly thought. Her real name was Tulula, but people had been calling her "Tulah" since she was a little girl. She was the prototypical young woman of the Roaring Twenties—a "flapper" in every sense of the word. She loved to go out with young men who had expensive, fast-moving cars. Last year's boyfriend, George McCarthy, drove a 1925 Chrysler Roadster. It was a two-seater convertible with beautiful large whitewalls and spiked wheels. It was one of the first sports cars. The best feature was the rumble seat. Tulah and George loved to double-date and have the other couple drive as they sat in the rumble seat hugging. They cruised the streets of Detroit in this exquisite roadster. Tulah and George did not last long as a couple after she met her newest heartthrob, Buster Kennedy. The first thing that caught her eye was Buster's brand-new 1928 Model A Ford Roadster. This was the most important Ford release since the release of the classic Model T.

Buster was a cocky young man. He had a mustache and combed his hair like Rudolph Valentino, the matinee idol of silent films. He loved his new Model A and loved to sit in the rumble seat with Tulah. As they walked in the door, Marvin could quickly tell that the "lightning bolt" had hit both of them. Holding hands, they made their grand entrance into the Arquette home.

"How are you doing?" Buster mumbled to Marvin.

"Very well, thanks. I just started my new job a few weeks ago, fixing those new Fords you like to drive." Marvin responded.

"Fords don't need much fixing. I fix my own, easy as can be," Buster replied with voice that was more of a whisper.

Buster was the type of person who always thought he knew as much or more about what other people did for a living as they knew themselves. He loved to try to convince people that he knew just about everything. He was gruff, a bit pretentious, yet a good-natured person. Tulah was attracted to his good looks, his braggadocio personality, and of course, to his Model A Roadster with the rumble seat.

Leaving Buster with Marvin, Tulah rapidly moved into the kitchen. Although taller, Tulah resembled Phyllis. She had a thin, aquiline face and a very thin frame. One could easily think he could easily wrap his thumb and finger around her wrists or ankles. She was constantly in motion—almost jittery. She instantly started picking up in the kitchen and cleaning the counters. She loved to clean. Her brothers and sisters called her a compulsive cleaner. "Compulsive" was a word now made popular with the interest in the new social science in vogue in the 1920s called "psychology."

Sigmund Freud was a household name now.

Tulah loved the idea of being a "flapper." She wore the clothes of the day with bobbed hair and makeup. She even would sneak a cigarette now and then. Her dress was baggy and exposed her arms and legs from the knees down. She turned down her hose to her ankles and powdered her knees, another new fad. She even had a new ankle bracelet just above her pumps. It was given to her by her new beau, Buster. She was the embodiment of the poem by Dorothy Parker entitled "The Flapper."

> The playful flapper here we see,
> The fairest of the fair,
> She's not what Grandmas used to be,
>
> You might say, au contraire.
> Her girlish ways may make a steer,
> Her manner cause a scene.

But there is more harm in her,
    Than in a submarine.
She nightly knocks for many a goal,
    The usual dancing men.
Her speech is great, but her control,
    Is something else again,
All spotlights focus on her pranks,
All tongues her prowess herald,
For which she well may render thanks
    To God and Scott Fitzgerald.
Her golden rule is plain enough,
Just get them young and treat them rough.

She said hello to her mother and asked if she could help with dinner. Her mother, smiling, said she had things under control. Quickly she returned to the parlor where Marvin and Buster were having an argument over the need for unions in the automobile plants.

Doris and Phyllis now joined the others in the parlor. They had been talking in their bedroom about their adventuresome day at Belle Isle. Phyllis wanted to talk about the brazen young man who had tried to cut in line.

Doris was now in high school. Her personality was much like Marvin's. Both always seemed to be happy. She had a pretty face, slightly rounder than that of her other sisters. She did not have the aquiline nose of her sisters. She was about five foot one, and also thin. She seemed pleased with who she was and was always willing to explore the exciting places in Detroit with her younger sister, Phyllis. Of the seven children, these two got along the best and were as much friends as sisters.

The two youngest siblings were Bobbie and Johnny. Bobbie was eight years old and Johnny was six. They were typical young boys who loved to play ball, ride bikes, and push and shove with the numerous boys their ages who lived in the neighborhood. Johnny was the most adventuresome and Bobbie the more serious, although their personalities were far from being shaped at this young age. They liked to follow Phyllis and seemed to view her as more their own age, as Phyllis was barely bigger than either of them.

The Tiger ball game blared on the new radio, another new invention that was becoming incredibly popular. Listening to the Tiger games was the perfect relaxation for William Arquette. His regular routine after work was to first put the ball game on the radio, pour a beer, and read the paper. Baseball was definitely America's pastime in 1928.

Dinner was always timed so that he could have about a half hour to relax first. Although it was illegal to manufacture and sell alcohol, many men in Detroit learned how to make their own. Also, it was very easy to get alcoholic beverages in Detroit, as Windsor, Canada, and Detroit served as a major conduit for bootleggers during the era of Prohibition. Statistics showed that fewer people drank alcohol during Prohibition than before it started, but it would be hard to prove this in Detroit.

Dinner was ready. Hanna Arquette had made a large kettle of Irish stew. Although the French culture was still prevalent in Detroit, it seemed to be losing its grip on the town. Very few families served quiche or other French dishes. As soon as dinner was ready, Phyllis began bossing everyone around. She always took control of social situations, and with Buster, Tulah, and Marvin back in the house, she had lots of arranging to do. Even her father would listen to her. She told everyone where to sit at the table and directed where the food was to be arranged. William was seated at the one end of the large dining room table. Hanna was in the center nearest the kitchen. Tulah and Buster were opposite William. Bobbie and Johnny sat together between Phyllis and Doris.

Soon the food was passed around and the family became quiet as they ate the delicious meal. Halfway through the meal the conversation began. It was Phyllis who started. She and Doris talked about their wonderful day at Belle Isle. Marvin talked about his new job and a girl he had just met. As he was somewhat shy by nature, it took a lot of probing questions to find out about her. Hanna Arquette tried delicately to ask questions about her religion, her family, and where she lived. Phyllis wanted to know about her politics, what she did, and what kind of person she was. She was very protective of her siblings, even at the young age of eleven. She always felt that sometimes Marvin was "too nice" and that he would fall for the first girl who showed interest.

Soon the conversation turned to automobiles. Buster wanted to impress William with his knowledge of cars. He talked in detail about his new Model A Roadster and how expensive it was. He described the intricacies of its engine and how easily he could fix it. William would try to correct him at times, but Buster would always insist he was right. Tulah was impressed with everything Buster said, but she didn't want to swoon too much; after all, she was a modern woman. Soon Tulah and Buster were talking about the night they had planned. They were going to the Gaylord Dance Hall, a trendy place in the Detroit nightlife.

Phyllis decided that they had spent enough time at the dinner table. She directed Marvin and Doris to help their mother with the dishes. She told the younger boys to go outside and get some exercise.

"Let's go listen to the ball game and read the newspaper, Daddy," she asked her father. Obligingly, he followed her into the parlor. This was a nightly routine when the game was on the radio. Reading the paper would become a daily activity for Phyllis the rest of her life. William Arquette clearly enjoyed his spunky daughter. They talked more like two adults than as adult and child.

Chapter 3

In August 1928, William O'Slattery, who was called Billie by his mother but Bill by everyone else, turned thirteen years old, but he looked and acted more like a sixteen- or seventeen-year-old. He was both admired by his friends and sometimes kidded by them because he was sometimes so serious. He had set his goals for the future. First, he wanted to become a part of what he saw was a dynamic, growing, vital, majestic automobile business. Second, he wanted to escape the poverty he was growing up in. Third, he did not want to fall into the problems that befell his father that were caused by alcoholism. Fourth, he knew he had to study and read and learn rather than simply play all the time. Fifth, he wanted to raise a family.

His father, Raymond Patrick O'Slattery, was a self-made man. He did not complete high school, but learned to be a master electrician. It was a great trade to have in the early part of the twentieth century in Detroit. Because of the burgeoning manufacturing business and the expansion of electricity all over the city and the nearby farms, a skilled electrician was in tremendous demand. Raymond rose quickly in his field. He became a leader in the Electrician's Union and was a high-ranking officer. Some say he was part of the so-called "Irish Mafia" in Detroit. However, it was never clear what that actually meant. Because of his power, many industrialists, city and county governments, small businesses, and others came to him to obtain the skilled workers they needed. Raymond had developed enormous power and prestige by 1920. In modern-day terms he was sort of a "godfather" in Detroit. He created a significant empire by providing jobs and favors. However, he said he never did two things. He never took kickbacks or sold jobs. In conversations with his son, Bill (as he called him), he always reminded him of this.

"If you get a good skill, handle people with respect and work hard; you never need to be dishonest," he would constantly remind his son, and Bill never forgot this advice.

Until 1920 Raymond O'Slattery had never drank alcohol. He constantly reminded his son of the "curse of the Irish." Raymond remembered the stories of the ruined families and businesses caused by alcohol abuse. He could trace his ancestry to County Cork, Ireland. They came to America during the infamous potato famine of the 1860s. They had seen firsthand how alcohol had hurt the modernization of the Irish people.

"Never, never, drink, Raymond," he was told hundreds of times.

Raymond O'Slattery had heeded this advice for most of his life. However, the mounting pressures of holding power, the constant requests for jobs, the endless hours at his work sites, made him weak on one fateful day. He was coerced by a group of his subcontractors to have one beer at O'Shaunessee's Pub on Gratiot Avenue. Unfortunately, he rationalized that one beer would not hurt. He drank the one beer, then another, and then another. He was drunk before he finished the first beer. He never came home that fateful night, and it began his fall from power. He began to go to pubs on a regular basis. He came home later and later at night. He neglected his family. He neglected his work. It was not that he drank a lot, people would say, but that he would have one drink and become instantly drunk. It was a genetically caused physiological reaction to alcohol that made him get drunk so fast. In this state, he lacked the willpower to say "no" to his friends when they implored him to have "just one more."

Soon Raymond was unable to keep up with the rigors of his job and his union position. He lost his former contracts, and it was difficult to find new contracts because the knowledge of his problem with alcohol was spreading throughout the electrician trade and the city. Even though Detroit was becoming larger, it still retained somewhat of a small-town culture and it was hard to keep secrets.

The O'Slatterys had a large house near Grand River Avenue and Livernois. During the mid-1920s, Raymond was still able to make a modest living by being an hourly worker, but his "kingdom" was now gone. When he would go on his more frequent "benders," he would get fired and have to find a new subcontractor to hire him. This was making it more and more difficult for the O'Slattery family.

Bill took the streetcar after leaving Belle Isle and then got a transfer and took a bus to Wyoming Avenue and Joy Road. He walked the last few blocks to his home. He was dirty and sweaty from the afternoon football game. His father had not started drinking and was sitting at their old piano. The radio was on and his father was playing the exact songs that he heard on the radio. He could not read a note of music, but he could play almost anything he heard. When he stopped playing, his fingers would shake because of the effects of alcohol after only a few years of drinking.

"Hi, Bill," he said as his son entered the house. "Looks like a little football again. Did you kick some butt, as usual?" he asked.

"Sure, Dad," he answered. "Where's Mom?"

"She is cleaning a neighbor's house again," he replied with a note of embarrassment in his voice.

Bill had one sibling. Her name was Rachel. She was nine years older than Bill and no longer lived at home. She had gotten married as a teenager because of love and out of a desire to escape a home life that had once been perfect but had become more and more depressing. Her husband, John, was ten years older. He was a swashbuckling, handsome young man, who earned his living as an electrician. He had obtained his job through his father-in-law, Raymond O'Slattery. John and Rachel already had a son and a daughter and were expecting another child.

Bill's mother returned from her cleaning job. She was a second-generation Irish woman. Her maiden name was Murphy, as were both her parents' surnames. Her name was Anne. Her husband was about five feet seven with a medium build. Anne was slightly taller and fairly robust in stature. She was somewhat muscular and very strong. Her son, Bill, received his stature from her. "Cream puff" was her favorite expression. "Don't eat your dinner and you will become a 'cream puff'"; "don't work hard and you will become a 'cream puff'"; "don't get out of bed early and you will become a 'cream puff'" were some of the things she would say.

Anne was working hard to cope with the problems that had befallen her husband. She loved him tremendously and admired the abilities, wisdom, and honesty he had shown before his disease. The prevailing thought in the 1920s was that alcoholism was the result of a weak character. People chose that path. However, Anne was an extremely intelligent woman who intuitively knew better. She had seen the disease in the Irish community and remembered the warnings given to her by her parents. She was determined to keep her small family together and determined to get her husband on the right path. And she was determined to not let this adversely affect her son. This became her passion.

Bill helped with the dinner and it was soon served. They sat down in silence. Bill most resembled his mother. Raymond was sober, but his hands continued to shake as he ate his dinner. Bill ate all of his dinner and asked for seconds. After all, he did not want to be called a "cream puff."

"Keep playing that football, Bill," Raymond said for the hundredth time. "It's your ticket to college. Soon college will become a necessity to make a good living. Get on the management side of things and pull the strings; unions are great but not that powerful, and they have to constantly fight for what they get. You know that I can get you a job as an electrician, but get into the other side of the game."

Bill had heard this often, but he often thought that the cards were stacked for him to end up an electrician. He was good with his hands and had good mechanical skills. Despite these practical thoughts, his dream was to work for Henry Ford.

"We'll get him through college. The new City College of Detroit will be affordable. We have to save some money," Anne interjected. She realized how gifted her son was and it was her dream to help make him a success. There were just too many opportunities in Detroit.

"There is going to be no better city in the world," Raymond added. "We have all the skilled people here to make this a dream city. We have the people with the ability to manufacture goods, to build parks, to build museums, to build opera houses, to make sports stadiums, and to solve almost all the problems of a growing city. Take advantage of that, Bill. There is one thing we have to come to grips with though. The white people and the colored people have to get along. We have to learn to live together. If the white people and the colored people divide and fight each other, Detroit will never reach its destiny." Raymond said this often. He was starting to forget what he had said the day before.

"Stay home tonight, Dad. Let's read and listen to the ball game," Bill begged. He knew that if Raymond went to the pub, he would not be home until it closed. It would be an even bet that he would not go to work the next day.

"Of course," he said. Anne looked sad and said nothing.

Bill and his mother cleared the table and went to the kitchen to wash the dishes. Raymond started playing the piano. It was amazing how good he was. However, after a few minutes, the music stopped, and Raymond disappeared. He could sneak out so quietly it was scary.

Anne kept washing dishes, and Bill walked to the living room. His eyes were sad, as he began to realize that he needed to grow up sooner than a young man should. As money problems mounted, the O'Slatterys were forced to sell more and more of their possessions. Anne loved to read, but she had to sell most of her books to buy food and other necessities. However, she kept a set of encyclopedias, an almanac, and several math books. She gave them to Bill. She recognized how gifted her son was and knew how much he wanted to be an automotive engineer and part of the dynamic industry. She never coaxed him to read, but she knew he would if she simply left the books around the house. Bill took one of the encyclopedias and walked out to the porch and started to read. Several neighborhood boys walked by and wanted Bill to hang out with them.

"No, thanks—just relaxing and reading a bit," he answered them. This had become a nightly ritual this summer. The kids laughed at him and called him a bookworm and "four-eyes." The hours of reading were taking a toll on his eyes. Anne had to clean several houses to be able to afford his glasses.

Amazingly, the O'Slatterys had been fairly wealthy a few years before. Their old house had three large bedrooms, two bathrooms (a luxury for the twenties), a parlor, and a dining room. It had been designed by Bill's father. He had installed most of the electricity, and his crews had put in the plumbing and other necessities.

Anne seemed not to let their new poverty bother her. She had an Irish wit and a touch of the blarney. Her optimism was maintained by her dreams for her son's future. Some argue that the Irish had failed to advance because of the church. The Catholic Church preached suffering on earth and rewards in heaven. She and others in Detroit were rejecting this philosophy as being flawed, and when they adopted the Protestant work ethic, they began to excel. This wonderful, vibrant city had many opportunities, and many Catholics were becoming convinced that a person could be happy on earth and in heaven. In fact, this was the way it should be, because it helped the individual, the family, and the community. She might not have total happiness in her lifetime, but she was convinced her son would find it.

Anne loved jokes and loved to laugh. Bill also did, but he maintained a serious demeanor promulgated by his need to succeed. He would not let a bunch of neighborhood kids get under his skin. The irony was that he was big enough and strong enough to knock their lights out. But this never entered his mind. Football seemed to be the perfect way to get rid of those negative feelings.

Chapter 4

The next day young Bill got up early. He often helped his father's "cousin" in his warehouse business. It was never certain if they were actually cousins. But they said they were. For sure they were great friends. Johnny O'Slattery was a tall, thin, craggy-faced former baseball player. He was about forty now, but he looked much older. His face was dark and leathery from the endless hours he spent on the sandlot baseball fields of Detroit. He still chewed tobacco and always carried a pop bottle to spit into. He played in the Tigers farm system for several years. He was fast with a great arm and was a natural center fielder. He never was a great hitter, but when he got a single he often stretched it into a double. A left-handed hitter, he perfected the drag bunt. If he did get on first, he often was able to steal second. At the age of twenty-six, he was on the verge of a major league career; however, he never liked the constant travel of baseball and simply wanted to live in Detroit. Most of all, he hated the constant drinking of the players. Like Anne, he understood the perils of alcohol. Ironically, when Prohibition started, he instantly saw how much money could be made from bootlegging. He saw the thousands of workers in the automobile plants and knew they would not give up their beer and whiskey.

Another, even bigger irony was that Henry Ford was a teetotaler, as were most of the executives he hired. At least, he thought they observed abstinence. Those conducting job interviews were required to ask prospective employees about their alcohol use. If someone was caught drinking, his job was in jeopardy. Ford envisioned a totally sober workforce. He did this for ethical reasons, but also because he felt the employees would be more productive and less likely to get sick and lose valuable time on the job.

Michigan was one of the first states to pass a prohibition law. In 1917 the Damon Act was passed in Michigan and the spigots on booze were supposed to be turned off. However, as some say, "the best-made plans of mice and men ..." The social reformers never took into account how close Detroit was to Canada and thus a quick and endless supply of alcohol. Anyone with a boat could quickly cross the Detroit River to Canada. And Toledo, Ohio, was less than an hour away. Alcohol could be obtained in Canada and quickly distributed through Ohio and the rest of the country.

"False floorboards in automobiles, second gas tanks, hidden compartments, even false bottomed shopping baskets and suitcases, not to mention camouflaged flasks and hot water bottles were all employed by the entrepreneurial and the thirsty as they navigated the Dixie Highway between Detroit and the Ohio border," wrote Jenny Nolan in *The Detroit News*. "It was a sort of dress rehearsal for the ingenuity and audacity for the much larger operations to come."

Judges and police took a lenient view of offenders. They went to the growing number of "blind pigs" in Detroit as much as anyone. In Detroit vernacular, "blind pigs" was the same as the nickname "speakeasies," which would be used in other parts of the country in the 1920s. In 1919 the Damon Act was ruled unconstitutional. In another ironic twist, Ohio made the manufacture and sale of alcohol illegal in the same year, and now the buckeyes drove to Detroit to partake.

And in keeping with the irony, the U.S. government decided to make the nation a citizenry of teetotalers. The Volstead Act became law in 1920, and the rumrunners in Detroit had already played their preseason games. They were ready to go with all the wrinkles already worked out.

The Detroit River is twenty-eight miles long and less than a mile across in many places. There are numerous small islands that made good stopping-off points and hiding places. It was easy to avoid the police boats that patrolled the river. In addition, there were numerous inlets, tall bushes, and other natural hiding places along its banks. During Prohibition, 75 percent of the illegal liquor coming into the United States came through the Detroit River, the St. Clair River, and Lake St. Clair. Small and large boats, sunken houseboats, barges, rowboats, fishing boats, underwater cable delivery systems, and even a pipeline were used to smuggle alcohol. An electrically controlled cable hauled metal cylinders filled with up to fifty gallons of booze from Peche Island to the foot of Alter Road in Detroit.

One favorite trick was to throw the liquor bottles off the boats and let them sink in the river. The bootleggers would hire young boys to dive in the river and fish out the bottles. They would be paid a few pennies for each bottle retrieved.

According to *The Detroit Free Press*, "Illegal liquor was the second biggest business in Detroit in 1929, just behind the automobile industry; and there were as many as 25,000 blind pigs in the Detroit area by the height of prohibition."

Johnny O'Slattery owned a large warehouse along the Detroit River about five miles downriver from Detroit. He had saved enough money to pay in cash. Most of the money was not from his salary, which was meager during his minor league career, but from gambling. He was said to be the best poker player in all of baseball. His mathematical mind enabled him to count cards and calculate the odds instantaneously. Most of all, he understood people. He knew when to bluff and when not to. He predicted that after World War I, the flow of goods between the United States and Europe would go back to that of prewar days and possibly increase. He started an import/export business that flourished. Johnny O'Slattery became a "player" in Detroit.

In 1928 Johnny was still in the "import/export" business, but it had changed. His warehouse had taken on a different look in the last decade. There were armed guards everywhere. Padlocks were on all the doors, windows were boarded up, and people circulated with very few smiles on their faces. It looked more like a fort now than the "friendly" import/export business of 1918.

Johnny hired his nephew, Bill, to help out in the warehouse. He wanted to help get extra money to his cousin, Raymond. Bill looked old enough to avoid the enforcers of child labor laws. Still being a bit naïve, he never quite understood what Uncle Johnny was actually doing. His work was to simply carry crates and boxes from one place to another. He had started doing this the summer before, and it had significantly contributed to his strength and endurance. This would prove extremely beneficial on the gridiron. He loved the physical labor and was happy he could give his mother the money. His father knew he sometimes worked with Johnny but never knew to what extent. The forgetfulness and neglectfulness of alcohol abuse were taking their toll. On a beautiful summer day, Bill arrived to work at Johnny's warehouse.

"Hey, Billie! How the hell are you?" Johnny asked.

"Great. Thanks again for the work. The family needs it," replied Bill. He liked his "uncle," but he had a hard time accepting his rough language and cocky nature. He appreciated the work, but wished he was old enough to get a job elsewhere.

"Billie, I need a favor tonight."

"Sure. Anything, Uncle Johnny," Bill responded.

"I need you to meet me here tonight around ten. We have some expensive auto parts coming in from Canada and we need extra help to unload them. They are very fragile. Can I count on you?" Johnny asked.

"Sure thing, but I have to talk to my mom first."

Bill returned home at about seven o'clock. His mother and father were not at home. There was a note on the dining room table from his mother saying she had a house to clean and that she would be back around 10:00 PM. Dinner was in the icebox. There was no sign of his father. He ate, washed the dishes, and began to read *The Detroit News*.

The Detroit News was the afternoon paper, and *The Detroit Free Press* was the morning paper. Both papers secretly agreed to share the market.

It was becoming dark in Detroit. Bill thought about his uncle's request and decided he should help him. He wrote a note to Mother explaining how his uncle had asked him for extra help. If she had been there, she would have not allowed him to go. With his father away on most nights, the subject of Johnny O'Slattery rarely came up. Both parents knew what Johnny had gotten into but simply ignored it, just as most Detroiters ignored what was going on in the bootlegging business. Anne allowed Bill to work days with Johnny, because she felt that his daytime import/export business was legitimate. Also, the family needed the money.

It was a clear, beautiful Michigan night. The winds had blown the smoke from the factories and the cars from the city. It was a full moon. Bill took the bus to Johnny's warehouse and got there around 9:45 PM. No one was around; maybe he had made a mistake. Bill was the type of kid that always arrived early. Uncle Johnny knew he would be there, knew he would work faster than most men, and knew he would not talk to outsiders. For some reason he did not worry about getting a young man in the type of trouble that could adversely affect the rest of his life.

Suddenly an old truck came screeching down the road. There were three men in it with Johnny riding shotgun. It halted in front of the warehouse. The other two men were red-faced Irishmen who had just come from one of the nearby blind pigs. Potbellied and rough-talking, they were the type of Irishmen that young Bill was starting to not like. He was proud of his Irish heritage and liked all their contributions to America. However, he was learning to not like the brash, hard-drinking, hard-fighting type of Irishman that hung out in illegal pubs. He wished his "uncle," and especially his father, would not hang out with this type. He sometimes told people he was part German because he admired the image they had as being more sober, hardworking, serious, and disciplined.

"Billie, glad you could come. Get in the back. We have a few miles to drive. We have to pick up some auto parts down by the docks … trying to save a little tax money," Johnny yelled to him.

Without saying a word, Bill jumped in the rear of the truck and off they sped. They wound their way through the streets of Detroit, stopping twice to make sure no one was following them. After about thirty minutes, they arrived at the Detroit River. Then they went off the paved road and followed bumpy dirt roads downriver. They stopped at one of the numerous coves on the river and waited behind some big elm trees.

After a few minutes they saw a light from the river. It was coming directly at them. No one was talking now, and their car lights were out. The boat docked and two men got out and came directly to the truck. Bill instantly could tell that all of this had been planned, but never in his wildest imagination would he think that there might be illegal alcohol on the boat. Johnny motioned to Bill and the other two men who came with him to come down to the dock. In the moonlight it was easy to see at least a dozen large wooden boxes on the rather large yacht. Johnny did not say anything. Bill and the two red-faced Irishmen boarded the yacht and started to unload the boxes. Johnny drove the truck closer. It took about ten minutes to carry the boxes from the yacht and load the back of the truck. Bill saw Johnny give something to the driver of the boat, and it immediately sped downriver.

The four got into the truck and slowly started to drive off. Just then, shots rang out, hitting the truck and making sharp dinging sounds as they hit the thick metal. Trucks in 1928 were made of thick steel. They more resembled World War I tanks than the trucks of later years. Several men came running toward the truck. One was firing a machine gun. Bill ducked as he sat in the cab of the truck. One of the bullets hit a box and a pungent-smelling liquid began pouring out.

"Holy shit! Get going, Johnny," yelled one of the Irishmen. Just then he was hit and blood spurted from his neck.

"Fuck! Floor it, Johnny," screamed the other. Without worrying about their cargo, Johnny sped away down the dirt roads and back to the highway. Bill could hear the glass breaking in the boxes and he now knew what this was all about.

Johnny sped directly to the hospital. "Purple Gang," he kept repeating to himself as he ignored all the stops on the streets. He had to save his buddy—the hell with the cops. Fortunately for them, no police were around. They went to the emergency room of the hospital and dropped off their friend. Without talking to anyone, the three took off. They did not want to answer any questions. The medical personnel took the wounded man inside. There was blood all over his clothes. It would be the last time they would ever see Sean O'Shaunessee, the owner of the blind pig that was Raymond O'Slattery's hangout.

Johnny drove back to the warehouse confident that no one was following him. The two men quickly unloaded the truck and locked the contents inside. Johnny told Mac, as he called him, to watch his back while he was going home. He then drove his nephew home. There was no conversation. He knew he had almost gotten his favorite nephew killed and knew he would never ask such a favor again.

Bill got out of the car several blocks from his home and walked through the alley home. It was close to midnight now. He quietly walked into his house. Anne was sitting on the porch. She was crying. Raymond was not home.

"Hi, Mom," was all Bill said as he walked through the house and went upstairs toward his bedroom. He washed briefly, changed out of his wet clothes, and jumped into bed.

Bill had grown up that night. He would never return to the warehouse and rarely saw his "Uncle" Johnny again. His mother never learned of the details of that night, but she was intuitively aware that Johnny had risked her son's life. However, she knew that Billie, her life, would never get involved again. She went to bed, crying herself to sleep.

Not having a job anymore, Billie decided to spend his free time in the library. His first day was spent going through newspaper after newspaper to find out more about the "Purple Gang." There was plenty in the papers about this notorious gang. He learned that a group of young "toughs," mostly Jewish, had graduated from petty street crime around Hastings Street to become a brutally vicious bootlegging crime organization. No one knew where the name came from. But legend had it that a Sammy "Purple" Cohen had given the gang its name. After World War I, Cohen's gang joined another nefarious group that called itself the Oakland Sugarhouse Gang. This gang was under the leadership of Abe, Ray, and Joe Bernstein. They had grown up in a section of Detroit called Little Jerusalem. They successfully transformed the "Purples" from a small-time gang whose activities mainly consisted of protection rackets and shoplifting into a well-oiled crime machine that had gained control of most of the liquor flowing into and out of Detroit.

The Purples also provided protection services for other bootleggers and served as a "policing" army to stop small-timers from smuggling booze across the Detroit and St. Clair Rivers. By the midtwenties, they had established ties with the Chicago syndicate of Al Capone and the St. Louis syndicate calling themselves the Egan's Rats Gang. The St. Louis connection provided a standing army to the Purples. The main purpose of this army was to keep Al Capone's people from invading their territory in eastern Michigan. The Purples were so brutal and so willing to use extreme levels of violence that even Al Capone did not challenge them. This was a spur in the side of Al Capone because he coveted the supply of booze to the thousands of industrial workers in southeast Michigan. The Purples also controlled drugs, gambling, and blind pigs in southeast Michigan—particularly the Detroit area.

It was this hornets' nest that Johnny O'Slattery stuck a stick into on that clear moonlit Detroit summer night in 1928. There was one good thing to come out of that night. Johnny returned to his legitimate import/export business. The owner of O'Shaunessee's blind pig was not so lucky.

The downfall of the Purples came in the early 1930s when they became involved in more and more kidnappings and extortion. As time went by, they suffered from internal assassinations and revolts. Also, numerous law enforcement agencies were able to infiltrate the gangs and eventually make numerous arrests. The famous federal agent Eliot Ness was involved in their demise.

Chapter 5

The next day, Doris and Phyllis got up early for a fun day downtown. The first part of their itinerary was to go to the Vernors ginger ale factory and store. Vernors is unique to Detroit. If you breathe in when you drink it, the gas goes up your nose and it is a weird sensation. Most Detroiters learn as children exactly how to drink it without this happening. When vanilla ice cream is added to Vernors, Detroiters call this a Boston cooler. No one exactly knows how Boston got into the name. (When root beer is added to vanilla ice cream, Detroiters call it a "brown cow.") The trip to the Vernors brewery is one of those things that helped make young and older Detroiters love their city.

The history of Vernors began in 1862. A young pharmacist named James Vernor wanted to invent a new type of ginger ale. He experimented with various recipes using gingerroot. He tried and tried but could not get it to suit him. He became a soldier in the Civil War and had to store his concoction in a charred oak cask. He returned four years later and almost threw it out. Before doing this, he courageously tasted the aged liquid and found it to be "deliciously different." Thus was born a brand-new beverage that would become an icon for Detroiters and those who visited the city.

In 1896 Vernor opened a plant on Woodward Avenue near the

Detroit River. This gave him the capacity to fill thousands of barrels with his now very popular "pop." "Pop" is a Michigan term for soft drinks. By 1915 the facility had expanded tremendously and he began bottling Vernors. Local artists painted golden-bearded "gnomes" and huge oak barrels to decorate the building and make it a tourist attraction for locals and visitors. It was a perfect stopping-off point before going to other popular places in Detroit like Bob-Lo Island.

The Arquette sisters got off the streetcar at the end of Woodward Avenue and walked straight to the Vernors fountain. The sisters both ordered Boston coolers. They also ordered a large bowl of potato chips. Better Made Potato Chips had just been founded and the company made a deal with the Vernor family to sell just this brand at the business. The two sisters ate and drank these Detroit delicacies with large smiles on their faces. They were so thin that if anyone was watching, they would encourage them to have several helpings.

Their next adventure was to go to Bob-Lo Island. Bob-Lo was another Detroit icon. It also has an incredibly interesting history. It is a small island about an hour by ferryboat from downtown Detroit. Its original name was *Etiowiteedannenti*, a name given to it by the Huron Indians, who once lived there. When the French occupied the island, they called it *Bois Blanc* because of the white wood of the trees that grew there. French priests established a Catholic mission on the island for the Huron Indians in the early 1700s. Fort Malden, a British military post, was built in Amherstburg, Canada, in 1796. This city was a short distance from the island. At that time, thousands of Native Americans encamped on the island in order to trade fur to the Americans and the Canadians.

The famous Shawnee leader Tecumseh made his headquarters on the island in the early 1800s. He sided with the British in the War of 1812 and made numerous attacks on American troops. It was a part of what has been called the Patriot War. In the 1830s a group of Canadians revolted against British rule. The Americans sided with the Canadians. It ended in a stalemate. During the American Civil

War, the island became part of the Underground Railroad. Escaped slaves hid on the island until they could safely make their way to mainland Canada.

Colonel Arthur Rankin bought 225 acres of the island from the Canadian government in the mid-1830s for the enormous price of $40. The remaining 14 acres were owned by Captain James Hackett, who was the lighthouse keeper. The lighthouse had been built in 1837. In 1869 the colonel sold the island to his son, Arthur McKee Rankin. He was a well-known star on the New York stage and went by the name of McKee Rankin. He built an elaborate estate on the island and stocked the land with deer, wild turkeys, and elk. He also had stables for his horses. He used the estate to host lavish New York–style parties and dinners. Unfortunately, when he got older and his stage career came to an end, the expensive parties bankrupted him.

The island was then sold to partners Colonel Atkinson and James A. Randall. Randall built a house from one of the British blockhouses that had been built during the War of 1812. Shortly after the sale, an infamous event occurred that created a national furor. His son, Tom Davey Randall, went duck hunting and disappeared during a violent storm. James hired spiritualists and numerous private detectives to find his son. Even séances were used. They searched throughout the winter. The body was found the next spring when the ice melted, but the mystery of his death was never solved. There are stories that the ghost of Tom Davey Randall still haunts the island.

The island was sold in the mid-1890s to the Detroit Belle Island and Windsor Ferry Company.

In 1898 the island was opened as a picnic and park area. Its natural beauty was astounding. Visitors began calling it "Bob-Lo Island." The name was officially adopted in 1929. It is approximately three miles long and one-half mile wide. It is eighteen miles downriver from downtown Detroit. It is just a five-minute ferry ride from Amherstburg, Ontario, Canada. The Canadian-owned Bob-Lo Excursion Line started a ferry service in 1898, and things were shaping up public use of the island. A limerick appeared in *The Detroit News* in 1900:

> *A maiden once said to her Pa,*
> *"Oh Pa, can I go to Bah Blah?"*
> *Her father said "No!"*
> *You can't go to Bob-lo,*
> *The place is too terribly far!"*

In 1902 and 1910 the steamers *Columbia* and *St. Claire* were built. They were exquisite and beautiful, and perfectly built for fun, relaxation, and romance. They could each hold over 2,500 passengers. Soon there would be amusement park–type attractions built on the island. However, the cruise to the island was as much fun as the destination for many, and a nice picnic was all that many wished for when they arrived on the island. Initially, the attractions were mostly simple, like the Ferris wheel and a carousel. It reflected the simple life Detroiters led at this time. In the early 1900s Henry Ford built a dance hall that was designed by Albert Kahn, a famous architect of the time. It was billed as the second largest dance hall in the world and the largest in North America.

During World War I, the Bob-Lo Excursion Line was still a Canadian-owned company. It was so important to America that U.S. military officials made an exception to the rule that draft-age men could not leave the country. They reasoned that it would be a hardship to young Michigan men to be forbidden to enjoy the island during the summer months. The boat ride downriver and a night at the huge dance hall was a romantic adventure for the young men and women of Detroit.

The second deck of the boats had beautiful dance floors that offered bands. During the big band era, the second decks rocked. Moonlight cruises were a big part of courtships in Detroit.

An icon of the Bob-Lo trip was Captain Bob-Lo (Joe Short). He was a diminutive ex-clown who had been hired away from the Ringling

Brothers Circus. He entertained children for decades and was ninety years old when he retired.

The two girls ran onto the boat. Their favorite seats were on the second deck alongside the dance hall. After they put their jackets and lunches on the seats they obtained, they ran to the railing and watched the majestic ship move down the river. The gigantic twirling paddles started rotating and the *Columbia* was off. They also loved to walk, run, and slide throughout the ship and the slick dance floor. It was a typical hot, humid Detroit summer day, but as long as it did not rain, the girls did not care.

They were standing on the deck, resting against the railings, watching the ship cut through the water when Phyllis said, "I so love this boat ride, Doris."

"Wouldn't it be romantic to go on a cruise with our boyfriends?" replied Doris. But at this time, going unescorted with a boy was still frowned upon. Even though mores were changing, they were still too young for that sort of thing.

"Someday I am going to do that. Maybe do it when it is dark, so we can watch the moonlight together," said Phyllis as she dreamed about her "Prince Charming." Although only eleven, she seemed to think and act like her older sister. They were inseparable during the lazy summer days and loved these excursions around the city they loved.

The music began in the dance hall. It was foxtrot-type music. Several couples started dancing. After a while, the music got faster and soon the couples were doing the "Charleston." The two sisters had had many dancing lessons and loved to do the modern-day dances of the twenties. They danced several Charlestons, with their legs going so fast they could hardly be seen. They were so thin and in such good physical shape that they could dance forever and barely get tired.

After about an hour, they arrived at Bob-Lo Island and immediately ran to one of the picnic areas. They had brought egg salad sandwiches, apples, potato chips, and some good ol' red pop. They were very hungry because of their dancing and quickly ate their lunches, enjoying the big, beautiful, tree-filled island. However, there was much to do and time was fleeing.

They quickly walked to the large carousel located in the center of the island. The carousel had big, colorful, beautifully carved wooden horses. They tried to get a different horse each time they went. The most fun was to try to catch the brass ring as they moved past it. The horses went up and down as they circled. Capturing the brass ring would get them a free ride. Being short, they were rarely able to get it; yet, this did not bother them, because it was so much fun. They screamed in delight as they went around and around. The music was the new-style Roaring Twenties music.

They seemed to have boundless energy as they rushed to the huge Henry Ford dance hall. Henry Ford had his signature on so many parts of Detroit. When they got there, they were again amazed at its size. It seemed to go on forever. Like they did on the boat, they loved to take off their shoes, run about twenty feet in their socks, and slide as far as they could. They did this for at least a half hour and then went to one of the soda fountains and ordered another red pop. There was nothing like a red pop to quench the thirst of two young, thirsty Detroit French girls on a hot day at Bob-Lo Island.

"To the Arquette sisters," they toasted as they enjoyed their delicious red pops.

Finally, they had to return to the *Columbia* for the trip home. They were silent as they watched the river and the beautiful foliage alongside. Phyllis again started dreaming about her future boyfriend and how they would enjoy this wonderful ride down the river—dance on the ship, dance on Bob-Lo Island, ride the carousel, return home holding hands on the deck as they silently smiled and thought about how much they loved each other and this marvelous city.

Tired, the girls returned home via the streetcar, buses, and walking. It was getting dark. The house seemed very quiet as they approached. With five other siblings, there rarely were periods of silence. Usually the two younger boys were playing outside at this time. As they entered the house, they sensed that something was wrong. Their father was sitting on a couch holding the hand of their mother. They were crying. The two younger boys had taken their baths and were in bed. Horrified, Phyllis asked what was wrong.

"Your mother has just returned from the doctor," William said softly.

"She has been complaining of pain in her stomach for several months now and she finally agreed to see the doctor." William could hardly get the words out. He so loved his sweet, happy, petite young wife.

Doris and Phyllis began to cry.

"What did the doctor say?" they asked in unison, barely able to get the words out. Intuitively they knew that something was terribly wrong. Their mother was rarely sad and without a smile on her face.

"He still has to do some tests, but he warned that it does not look good. We all have to be strong and pray for your mother. We all have to do more work until she gets better." He was being optimistic.

Chapter 6

In the fall of 1928 there was still optimism in Detroit, but there was a strange feeling that permeated the air. Gang activities were getting more and more brutal. The Model T and other Ford cars were not selling as well. There had been overproduction, and, ironically, Ford was suffering because of its own excellence. The Ford cars were built so well and were so easy to fix that people could keep them for a lifetime. Planned obsolescence was being introduced by other car makers but not by Ford. It seemed liked the Roaring Twenties were losing their roar.

There was a dark cloud hanging over the Arquette family. Hanna Arquette had been diagnosed with cancer of the uterus. Being little and frail, she would be unable to fight much longer. William Arquette was so devastated that he could barely go to work. The oldest children rarely visited. Doris was continuing to study hard to get through the High School of Commerce. She knew she would need to get a job as soon as she could. She tried to become the mother of the household, but it was not practical at this time. Her priority was to get through school and to become independent.

Phyllis, now almost twelve, was entering the second half of the seventh grade. She had grown slightly—almost four feet ten inches now—but she was still very thin, weighing barely seventy-five pounds.

She was changing into a woman, but still did not look much older than ten years old. When Doris was home, she and Phyllis would share the household duties. But eventually Phyllis assumed command of the situation. Being a natural leader and organizer, she was very comfortable telling others what to do and was able to do it in such a way that others still liked her. She made sure her father was off to work on time, washed and ironed clothes, fixed most of the meals, cleaned the house, and, most of all, looked after the two younger boys. She was forced to grow up early, but she never lost her idealism and optimism. She had enough energy for the entire family and simply knew that she had to keep this family together. She never complained and managed to retain the child within.

Bobbie and Johnny were confused and sad because of the illness of their mother. At their age, it was extremely difficult to understand what was happening. This time period would affect their personalities the remainder of their lives.

Hanna loved the holidays and spent much of her remaining energy planning for Thanksgiving and Christmas. The Arquette family had money for presents, but it could not make up for the sadness emanating from the illness of their mother. She especially loved Christmas. In past years, she had spoiled her children with more presents than the household could afford. The younger boys were beginning to become dependent on their sisters, especially Phyllis. Though barely bigger than them, she protected and nurtured them. They often followed Phyllis wherever she went; yet they were typical boys who loved to play and roughhouse.

Soon, Phyllis would make school her refuge and savior.

Chapter 7

Bill O'Slattery was thirteen when he started eighth grade at the new Mackenzie Intermediate School, which would soon become Mackenzie High School. He was one of the biggest boys in his class, looking more like a tenth-grader than an eighth-grader. His voice had deepened, and he had begun to shave.

Like it would be for Phyllis, Mackenzie High School would be the savior and launching pad for him. It also allowed him to escape an unhappy home situation. It was the perfect place to allow two gifted children to excel.

The construction of Mackenzie started in the spring of 1928, and the school was opened by that fall. The school was named after the well-known, very popular, and very competent principal of Detroit Central High School, David Mackenzie. He was the motivating force behind the starting of a two-year college on the grounds of Central High. Initially, it was a two-year college called the City College of Detroit. Later, it became the prestigious Wayne State University.

Years later, the following was written in an alumni letter:

> In September of 1928, the new school opened its doors to a motley crew of expectant students, some of whom, perhaps, expected a gay time because of

the confusion which might possibly arise in a newly organized building. But order came more quickly than anyone expected, and in September, 1928, the first teachers' meeting was held in the shop, room 115, for that was the only room in the school in which there were chairs.

The first semester, the school waited patiently for the arrival of furniture. On the floor sat seventh, eighth and ninth grade students, in the rooms which now made up the south central section of the school, the only part of Mackenzie built for the first term.

Just one year after the opening of the school for its first classes, the second unit of twelve rooms on the west corridor was added to the portions already standing. There was much rejoicing at this step because of the decided improvement in lunchroom facilities. Previous to this time the lunchroom staff had wheeled the food into the corridors, where the students made their choices and then carried their lunches back into their respective homerooms. Now that this section had been built, room 119, which was one of the new rooms, was used as a serving room. The food, however, was still brought over from Cooley High School in large cans. In 1931, when the north section of the school was finally built, Mackenzie had a lunchroom and kitchen of its own. No longer was the transporting of food from school to school through the halls necessary.

During the first year, the men's room was the scene of band practice; football rallies were carried out in the halls. The first dances were held in the corridors of the third floor.

In 1932, when the first class graduated, Mackenzie was pretty much as it is today. Although it was intended to be a senior high school, it operated for quite a while as an intermediate: a half grade was added each term until it was full four year senior high school.

(At that time in Detroit students could start in the fall or in midyear; thus, for instance there would be 9A and 9B classes. This created two graduations per year.)

Mackenzie was like heaven for Bill O'Slattery. The stock market had not yet crashed, and there was much optimism and enthusiasm in the new students. He entered his first year as if on a mission. He wanted to be the best student and the best athlete in this class. He realized early in life that academics and football would be his hope for the future. Bill would sit in the front row of every class. This was because he was so enthusiastic and because his eyes were not good due to the constant reading of the books he had at home. He had read the entire encyclopedia many times over. When he was forced to sit in alphabetical order, he did not object, because Natalie was usually next to him.

After school, it was time for the first football practice of the year. Bill O'Slattery had been thinking about this for years. He loved football, especially the contact part—the blocking and tackling. He was six feet tall and weighed over 170 pounds, which was very big for 1928. Mackenzie was a small school at this time, but at least half the boys went out for the team. Detroiters had always loved football. Because of the great teams of the University of Michigan, most young boys dreamed about excelling in football. Young boys played sandlot baseball until the fall and then played sandlot football until it was too cold. The helmets were made of leather and the thin pads were sewn into the uniforms. There were few rules at this time, and when the going got tough, it was not unusual for a player to throw his helmet aside.

Their coach was Alan Leahy and he had a one assistant coach, Frank LaRue. They looked out at about one hundred eighth and ninth-grade boys. They were pleased by the number of boys, but not too pleased with their size. Coach Leahy blew his whistle and screamed at them to gather around him. Since they didn't have upper grades in the school, their first two years would be jayvee only.

"All right, everyone take a knee!" he yelled.

"Welcome to the first jayvee football team at Mackenzie. I am Coach Leahy and my assistant is Coach LaRue. Coach and I have been together for ten years now. We coached at Redford High School before coming here, and I am sure you know about their powerful teams. You will be beating them before long. If you are willing to work your butts off, I guarantee it. Gentlemen, football is not for the weak of heart. We don't need quitters or complainers. Coach and I will not let you quit. 'Quitters never win and winners never quit.' You will work hard and there will be times you will not enjoy our practices. But in the end you will be proud that you had the guts to stay. Wanting to win is everything. When you rack up the victories, you will be proud of the hard work you have done to achieve them. You have a unique opportunity. You are on a school team that has never played before, and you can achieve far more than anyone would expect. This is America, gentlemen. In America we get up in the morning, we go to work, and we solve problems. This is true in football as much as anything you will ever do. Losing is not acceptable. Is that understood?" he yelled.

The squad was slightly mesmerized and barely answered the question. Coach Leahy bellowed out again, "Losing is not acceptable. Is that understood?"

This time the entire squad screamed, "Yes, Coach!" Bill O'Slattery yelled the loudest.

"Okay, gentlemen, I want the eighth-graders to go with coach LaRue and the ninth-graders to go with me." Bill O'Slattery jumped up and bolted forward like a thoroughbred from the gates. He ran as fast as he could to Coach LaRue, almost knocking him over.

"I said ninth-graders with me, young man," Coach Leahy yelled out at Bill.

"Yes, Coach. I heard you. I am in eighth grade," Bill responded.

Coach Leahy stared at him for a second, looked at the other players, and quickly said, "You are an exception today. You are with the ninth-graders."

"Yes, Coach. Sure thing," Bill replied as he sprinted toward him.

The coach laughed and thought, *We have a diamond in the rough here.*

The warm-ups were brutal. They did jumping jacks, push-ups, leg raises, sit-ups, grass drills (running in place and then jumping to the ground for more push-ups), and finally some sprints. More wind sprints would be at the end of practice. Next, the two grades were broken up into linemen and backs. The players were able to choose their positions. Bill O'Slattery immediately started to go with the linemen, but Coach Leahy told him to line up as a fullback. This was the only time he would look less than enthusiastic.

"What's wrong?" he asked.

"Well, I love to block and tackle and love playing center. I'm good at it. You'll see, Coach," Bill responded. Coach acquiesced.

It was the first and last time Coach Leahy and Bill O'Slattery would have a disagreement. From Bill's first sprint at Coach LaRue to his last days at Mackenzie, Coach Leahy and Bill O'Slattery formed a bond that would help to make Mackenzie High School a football powerhouse in a few short years.

The practice was frantic. Football was simple in 1928. Blocking and tackling and speedy backs were the heart of the game. All the drills were live, meaning full-out. Bill ran everywhere on his first day, and this would be his modus operandi his entire football career. If the coach said "go over there," he was the first to move. If someone needed Band-Aids, he would sprint to get some; if the coach was forming a scrimmage, he was the first to line up. He exhausted his teammates, but they looked at him as their leader. He was the one who would do the dirty work in the football trenches. They knew he would be first to the ball carrier when on defense. When the pressure was on, he would get better, meaner, and more focused. They knew this from his days on the sandlots of Detroit and the green fields at Belle Isle.

It was starting to get dark, but Coach Leahy wanted a short scrimmage. He placed the ninth-graders on offense and the eighth-graders on defense. He looked at Bill O'Slattery and motioned him to play defense. The first plays they learned were simple. Run off tackle to the right, run off tackle to the left, run around the left end, run around the right end, and a short pass to keep the defense honest. He mixed these up to make sure the defense could not guess the next play.

"All right, I want a person at every position," he barked out. He wanted to see those who wanted to immediately get into the action. He smiled slightly when he saw Bill immediately go to what they called the "roving center" position. Today, it is called a middle linebacker. It was a critical position in the running game of the era.

O'Slattery was in on almost every tackle. He smashed through ninth-graders like he was a senior. When a pass was called, he somehow sensed it and was able to knock it down; and even one time, he had an interception.

After this, they did ten wind sprints. Exhausted, the players took a knee around the coach.

"Gentlemen, I was pleased with what I saw today. We will be champions. And I do not want anyone quitting. Is that clear?"

They all screamed, "Yes!"

The coaches were pleased after their first practice. They knew they had an undersized line and average backs, but they knew they had a special player that could lead them to victories. They had coached at Redford High School through some fantastic years, but they were not retained this year. They wanted to show the people at Redford that they had made a big mistake.

Chapter 8

"He was a person who signed his name with an *X*."

Phyllis Arquette loved school and excelled at all subjects except math. She was the type of student that every teacher loved to have, and the class loved to have her there because she made school much more interesting. She was spunky, alive, intelligent, and a gifted speaker. She gave speeches and presentations as if she were onstage. It was school that made her forget the extreme sadness and loneliness she felt after the death of her mother.

Hanna Arquette had passed away shortly after Christmas. The cancer had spread quickly through her body, and she passed away in her sleep. William Arquette was completely distraught and had lost his zest for work. He worked fewer and fewer hours per week, and the family was having economic troubles. Donald, Marvin and Tulah had moved out of the house, so it was left to Doris and Phyllis to run the household. At first, the two younger boys were unable to help much. The sisters took them under their wings. Doris was closer to moving out of the home, so Phyllis continued to care for her brothers. The boys adored both sisters, treating them like their mothers now.

Phyllis continued to wash and iron their clothes, prepared their baths, made sure they were dressed for school, made their school lunches, prepared their breakfasts, cooked their evening meals, and put them to bed at night. She and Doris took turns reading to them. Their father wanted to help but was so depressed most of the time that he could not offer much help. He felt the solution to the home situation was to find another wife as quickly as possible. This was the way of life at that time. A widower wanted to immediately find another custodian of the house. Love was not always part of the equation.

Phyllis particularly liked history because she loved to debate. She would read the newspaper every day and use the information to promote class discussions and debate. Mr. Rhodes, the history teacher, loved the Civil War era and it became one of the major units for this school year. In 1928 there were still people living who had fought in that horrible war. His first assignment was for his student was to see if they could find a relative or an acquaintance that had been in the war and to write a speech about his/her experiences. Phyllis loved this assignment, because she had always marveled at the stories told to her when she was younger by her Grandfather Donald (Donnie) Arquette. She was full of pride when she started to tell the story of Grandpa Arquette.

"I want to tell you the story of my Grandpa Arquette. His first name was Donald, but he always went by Donnie. He was a Civil War hero. I so loved talking to him when I was only four or five. He had very thin bones with a thin, gaunt face. He had piercing blue eyes. He had high cheekbones, which he always said was because he was part Indian. He was seventy-six years old when he died. He could barely see, walked with a limp, and his hands shook. These were all from his Civil War injuries. He was very kind and truly loved his grandchildren, but I think I was his favorite because I loved to listen to his stories. He liked to show me the Confederate sword that he had found on one of battlefields on which he had fought. He loved the beautifully engraved, shiny sword." Phyllis began her story. She bounded around the room as she talked and showed all the students this magnificent sword.

"Grandpa was born in 1848 in Romulus. He was barely five feet tall. So can you see why I am such a shrimp?" (The class laughed)

Mr. Rhodes knew he would not have to do much teaching this period. Phyllis had taken over. She always seemed to take over a room. "She was little, but made herself heard," was a note in one of her later yearbooks. As she talked, Mr. Rhodes kept thinking this little girl could break barriers. She came to school in old clothes, with only a few pennies in her pocket. He noticed her and her sister walking their two younger brothers to grammar school. As the years went by, it would be her alone. With her blonde curls and easy smile, she could charm anyone. He noticed as she yelled at her brothers when it was necessary, laughed with them, talked to them, disciplined them, and gave them love. If she were a man, the doors of opportunity would have been wide open for her.

Phyllis continued enthusiastically, "Grandpa Donnie had little formal education and could neither read nor write when he enlisted in the Civil War. He had to sign his name with an *X*. He wanted to be a farmer. He told me he liked the hard work of farming and how satisfying it was when the harvest was ready and it was time for a little fun. He joined the Union Army in spring 1862, less than a year after the war started. He was assigned to Company E, 15th Michigan Infantry Volunteers. He was trained in Romulus and was sent to the western front of the war with his first deployment in Alabama.

"Grandpa took to soldiering, as he was an avid hunter and was able to track animals as well as anyone. He liked to camp in the woods and could live off the land. This made him perfectly suited for the upcoming war. He was fantastic at reconnaissance, spying on the enemy, and foraging," she continued.

Despite being a month shy of being twelve years old, she seemed to transform into an adult as she talked. Her "child" was being suppressed more and more as her family situation kept deteriorating. Although she never showed it, she had deep feelings of despair over her new role in life. She wanted to remain the girl who loved Belle Isle, streetcar rides, riverboat rides to Bob-Lo, and trips to Vernors to have brown cows and

Boston coolers. She would continue to do these things with Doris and her younger brothers, but she was now assuming the role of a mother.

"My grandpa was both one of the best soldiers and one of the most unlucky soldiers of all time. He was in dozens and dozens of battles and always fought bravely, but his career was spotted by bad luck and false accusations, and he had to fight for his honor the rest of his life.

"His first unlucky experience occurred shortly after becoming a soldier. He was in Alabama and was standing watch with several other soldiers. As he was standing there, a revolver of a soldier standing next to him accidently discharged and the bullet smashed through his hand. He did not want the other soldier to get into trouble, so he told his commanding officers that he had accidently shot himself. In wars throughout history, this was done by some soldiers to get out of their enlistments. He was court-martialed and found guilty and was in danger of being hanged as a coward. Finally, the other soldier told what had happened; however, they still did not believe him, thinking the other soldier was his friend and wanted to help him. After he spent some time in a makeshift stockade, they finally believed what had actually happened. His hand eventually recovered and he returned to duty, although, in his later years, his left hand would shake constantly.

"After returning to his unit, he fought in numerous battles in Alabama and Georgia. The soldiers at that time would march all day and night. When they met the other army, they would all meticulously line up on both sides of a big field with artillery set and then slowly walk toward each other as they fired their weapons. They were still using Napoleonic methods of warfare with modern-day accurate rifles. It was mass slaughter. Battles lasted for hours or until one side retreated. Battles were sometimes months apart because there were so many casualties. In the Civil War there were over six hundred thousand deaths and many, many more who lost a limb or had disabilities that haunted them the rest of their lives. I would have hidden behind a tree or dug a hole to jump in, but back then this was cowardly. Hundreds would be killed in a matter of minutes. Grandpa never talked about the specifics of the battles. He just shook his head and said it was 'terrible, terrible, and terrible— like the gates of hell opening up.'

"Grandpa Donnie's next big scare came in July 1864 in Centreville, Georgia. It was a battle in the middle of a big field. His luck was bad again. Canons opened up on both sides before they started their death marches. Imagine how scared you would be. I mean, why did they fight like this? Why didn't they all just start running? Of course, one reason was that their own officers would sometimes shoot them. Anyway, my grandpa was shot in his side and shot in his right hand this time. He was left for dead on the battlefield. The armies moved on and somehow he was not accounted for. He was delirious as he regained consciousness and started crawling to get away from the stink of the battlefield. Grandpa thought he would surely die, as he was unable to stop the bleeding. Almost all the soldiers thought they would never return home, so he was resigned to die as he passed out. Miraculously he woke up to the sound of Yankee soldiers. They had been out spying on the enemy. He was so weak he was unable to talk, and the next thing he knew he was in an army hospital."

The class was almost hypnotized by the story. She showed them pictures of her grandfather in his scruffy blue uniform and the blue hats they wore. He looked scrawny and haggard in the pictures. He had a long mustache, long sideburns, either a pipe or chew in his mouth, and a uniform that looked several sizes too big. But he also looked like the proud hero that he was. He looked sad, exhausted, and aged far beyond his years.

"Poor Grandpa! When he did not return to his Michigan unit and after not showing up for muster for over a month, he was officially made a deserter. His life was not worth much now. He could be shot by a Rebel bullet or a Yankee bullet. After a while, he was given a dishonorable discharge. Well, finally his wounds healed and he was able to start talking. He told the hospital staff what unit he was from and tried to convince them of his story. He did and he was allowed to return to his unit. After a lengthy court-martial, he was cleared of being a deserter. Unbelievably, he reenlisted and returned to his unit. Unfortunately, all of the falsehoods would be written down on his records and they would haunt him all his life.

"His unit soon became part of the march to the sea and the siege of Atlanta. Toward the end of the war the North decided on the new strategy of what they called 'total war.' The object was to break the will of the citizens. General William Tecumseh Sherman led this new policy. Sherman's middle name came from the famous Indian chief who once controlled parts of Michigan. Grandpa Donnie told me how difficult this was. They were cut off from their supply lines because they had to move so fast. They were like the invading armies of Genghis Khan in Asia and Europe. (Do you remember studying him last year in our world history course?) They would attack every Rebel they saw, and take over farms in order to obtain food. This had always bothered him because his family had been farmers. He knew how much work went into growing the crops and tending to the livestock. He always told me how sad he was about this horrible war. I always sensed he had feelings of guilt. Sometimes he told me he felt like he was fighting his cousins, not his enemy. He never totally understood what the war was all about. He knew that slavery was a part of it, but he also knew that there was much more to it. However, he would say that he felt it was his duty to fight and that they had to do what it would take to win.

"Since he was so good at foraging and hunting, his main duty was to be part of a squad that went far ahead of the main armies to find out where food was and where the enemy was. He liked this because he said it was much better than shooting at people. I asked him how many of the enemy he had killed and he would always took downward and be quiet. One time, he said he never knew for sure, but he fired into the line of so many charging soldiers that the odds were he shot some of the enemy 'These were Americans we were shooting at, and mostly poor Americans,' he told me sometimes.

"October 30, 1864, was a horrible day for Grandpa Donnie. His squad was foraging near Rome, Georgia, when they were attacked by a 'beehive of Rebels.' Those were his words. Within seconds, gunshots ripped through the flesh of his fellow soldiers. They were dead within seconds. Blood splattered all over him as he hit the ground to shoot back. They thought he had been shot also. This saved his life because he froze and pretended to be dead. The soldiers started taking their guns, boots, and any other things that could help them. When a soldier started taking off Grandpa's boots, Grandpa moved and this almost cost him his life. One of them pointed a pistol between his eyes. He had a smile on his face. Grandpa said he would never forget how he looked at him. He remembered his weathered face, his tobacco-stained, brown teeth, and his smell. Their eyes met and somehow they connected at a deeper level. The soldier stopped smiling and a sense of sadness came over him. It was as if they were brothers, both having suffered and survived through this horrible war. He never shot. Instead, he told him to get up and that he had to surrender his weapon and come with them. Grandpa was both lucky that day and unlucky, as he was now on his way to a prisoner of war camp. He had heard about how these camps were worse than hell.

"Within a month Grandpa had been transported to a prisoner of war camp in Vicksburg, Mississippi. When he arrived, he was in decent health. By the time he left this 'hell-hole,' as he called it, he had contracted an eye disease that would make him almost totally blind. When he finally left this camp near the end of the war, his body was covered with sores, he had severe dysentery from worms in his intestines, and he was a walking skeleton. But he survived.

"Since he was not accounted for on the battlefield, his unit had declared him a deserter and a traitor. He had also been charged with aiding and abetting the enemy. He found out about those charges when he was returned to his unit. Again he had to prove his innocence. A trial was convened, and fortunately the court-martial judges said they believed his story and he was found not guilty. He was never sure if they believed him or not. His take on it was that everyone was tired of killing and that when they looked at his blindness and his emaciated body, they took pity on him.

"The fighting part of the war was over for Grandpa Donnie. He was an unbelievable hero, courageous beyond belief. Just think, he could have gotten out of the war after he was accidently shot with a pistol. But he reenlisted and it caused him to suffer for the rest of his life. For the remainder of his life he would have to fight for the meager pension that Congress gave to disabled soldiers. Every time he went to renew the pension, the falsehoods about his career were brought up. Fortunately, each time he was able to vindicate himself. There were even times when he was accused of faking his blindness, and he had to go to a doctor each time to prove he was not.

"After the war, he returned to Romulus and tried to get work. He sometimes would work as a farm laborer, or a mechanic, or simply as a hired hand, but he never held a steady job. He lived the rest of his life off the pension from the government. However, he was still able to marry and raise a family.

"Five years after his discharge from the army Grandpa Donnie got married. This marriage certificate indicates his wife, Caroline Hinshing, was seventeen years old. But these other documents (Phyllis showed the class the other documents) show she was actually just over thirteen years old. That wasn't much older than most of you are, but at that time girls got married at a very young age and there were no laws against it. Grandpa was twenty-two at the time. She was even shorter than my grandpa, so you can really see why I am such a shrimp." (The class laughed as they had before.)

"Grandpa Donnie and Grandma Caroline had five children. The second oldest was my father, William Arquette.

"So that is the story of my Grandpa Arquette. He was a true hero, yet he never received any medals or thanks for the sacrifices he made to keep the Union together and ultimately to get rid of slavery. There were thousands like him during the Civil War. I hope you enjoyed his story." She then showed the class all the documents that proved all this had actually happened. The class applauded and Mr. Rhodes gave her an *A* for the assignment and was very pleased. He was truly moved by the story of Corporal Donnie Arquette, a person who signed his name with an *X*.

Chapter 9

"Detroit had suffered, struggled and survived the Great Depression with ingenuity, generosity, pride and grit." *The Detroit News*

When Phyllis and Bill entered school in the fall of 1929, the U.S. economy and the economy of Detroit were seriously slumping. Fewer and fewer cars were being manufactured and there were massive plant layoffs. This had a ripple effect throughout Michigan and the entire country. The country was becoming more and more dependent on the automotive industry.

In October 1929, the stock market crashed. Even though some people think the crash caused the Great Depression, most experts agree it was just a precursor of things to come. In truth there were multiple causes. Some list the following as causes: Europe was also in a slowdown; the Federal Reserve failed to help failing banks; the government failed to follow the rules of the gold standard; the government increased tariffs by record amounts, thus causing trade wars; the government reduced the money supply; the Hoover administration raised taxes; there were no safety nets; pessimism was spreading; there was a run on banks; record droughts hurt farmers in the West; investors were engaging in reckless speculation in stocks and land; investors were buying on margin in the stock markets; factories were overproducing; and some others. Regardless of the causes, it hit Detroit extremely hard because the city was so dependent on manufacturing and the sale of its goods. Of the causes listed above, many say it was overproduction that hurt Detroit the most. In a sense, Detroit was a microcosm of the country. Its struggles and its fight to get out of the deep hole were examples of how Americans will never give up. It showed how people tried to help themselves rather than immediately turn to the government to bail them out.

As for everyone else, the lives of Phyllis Arquette and Bill O'Slattery were affected by the Depression. However, the fact that they spent a great deal of time in high school helped them to escape some of its rages.

The following is information included in articles in *The Detroit News*. It gives a good picture of Detroit at this time and how the people reacted.

The 1920s had been a glorious time for Detroit. By the end of the decade, Detroit was producing approximately 5.4 million cars and trucks a year. The cars and trucks were being sold all over the United States. The horse-and-buggy days were over. The money that flowed in enabled Detroit to build and grow. Several of its most famous, tallest, and most spectacular skyscrapers were built during this decade. These included the Penobscot Building and the Fisher Building. The Detroit Zoo opened and became one of America's best zoos. The Detroit-Windsor Tunnel opened to cars, enabling people to drive under the Detroit River to Canada. The Covered Wagon Company of Detroit began building what they called "trailer coaches," which were later called "mobile homes."

Bill O'Slattery was in ninth grade and Phyllis Arquette was in the second half of eighth grade at Mackenzie High School (it now called itself a high school) when the stock market crashed in 1929. Within a year car companies were producing three million fewer cars and trucks than they had produced in 1928. The loss of jobs was immediate and staggering. In addition, the automobile industry had created many satellite companies around Detroit and there were giant ripple effects on these jobs. This hurt many businesses throughout Michigan, Ohio, and Canada.

One important thing that made the Great Depression even worse than recessions in later times was our cultural differences. In the 1920s and 1930s most families had one person working, usually the man. So when that person was laid off, the entire family was without a paycheck. Later in our history, women entered the workforce and many families would have two people bringing home a paycheck; therefore, 20 percent unemployment was much worse in 1932 than it would have been later in our history.

By 1930, Prohibition had been in effect for a decade. Ironically, bootlegging was one of Detroit's only businesses to thrive. More bootlegging operations sprung up and more blind pigs were opened. This had another adverse effect on Detroit, as there were more gangs and more gang warfare. A vivid example occurred in the month of July 1930. The month was called "Bloody July" after ten murders were committed by gangsters. In another example, anti-mob radio commentator Jerry Buckley was killed as he sat in the lobby of the LaSalle Hotel.

Unemployment became the biggest problem. On September 25, 1930, Detroit opened registration offices for the unemployed. On that day, 19,412 jobless registered. By the end of the next day the list had grown to 46,314, and by the end of the month, 75,704 had registered.

However, Detroit was a resilient city. Detroiters immediately tried to help those who needed help. Detroit represented the very essence of the American spirit and the American idea. Self-reliance, initiative, optimism, resourcefulness, inventiveness, and the work ethic would be the engines of Detroit's recovery.

The following is from an article in *The Detroit News* that was entitled, "How the Great Depression Changed Detroit."

> In 1930 the Mayor's Commission on Unemployed
> came up with the idea of the jobless becoming apple
> vendors. The idea came from a similar plan in New

York City. Veterans and men with dependents were eligible. Apples were bought from Washington State growers directly at the produce terminal and sold at 5 cents each. Vendors had to pay for the first box, which was under two dollars. Vendors were licensed and had to be Detroiters with at least one year of residence, and were assigned to specific locations. Some 11,000 apples were sold the first day, November 24th by 150 vendors. Busy corners were rotated so that one man didn't have the best spot. At one time there were 700 apple vendors.

In Detroit as well as in other cities, there was a Catholic group called the Capuchins. This was short for the Capuchin Franciscan Province of St. Joseph. This was a community of friars inspired by St. Francis of Assisi. Their goal was "to transform the world through Reverence …" They sought to do the following: "We preach, teach, cook and counsel. We minister in hospitals, schools, soup kitchens, parishes, and in the mission field. We are pastors, artists, missionaries, farmers, mechanics, and writers." They were one of the groups that helped Americans survive the horrible times. By November 1930, the Capuchins were feeding eight hundred people a day.

In other examples of people helping people, the Fisher brothers (they were Detroit industrialists) provided shelter for twenty-five hundred homeless men in their Fisher Plant at Fort and 23rd Streets. The White Tower Restaurants, a Detroit icon and precursor to fast-food restaurants, served free lunches on Christmas and other holidays.

By 1931 the situation was becoming critical. There were demonstrations in front of city hall on January 2. Auto production went down to 1,332,000 vehicles in 1931. The Fisher plant, one of the chief assembly plants in Detroit, totally stopped production and now became the City Municipal Lodging House. It had heat, lights, showers, meals, and bunks for the homeless. With the despair, however, the crime rate actually went down. As joblessness went up, kindness also went up.

There were many charitable donations and activities. Senator James Couzens donated $200,000 and Louis Mendelsohn donated $100,000. These were fortunes at that time. Rosenberg's Department Store delivered thousands of food baskets, and J. L. Hudson's contributed significant sums of money. As many as sixteen hundred physicians donated free medical care under the auspices of the Medical Relief Committee. Acreage was donated by businesses and families to the "thrift gardens." There were 4,369 gardens the first year, and by 1933 there were over 7,000.

Clothing drives were always in progress. They were organized by police, churches, businesses, charitable organizations, and schools. The Red Cross contributed 1.2 million yards of fabric in September 1932. The Detroit Red Wing hockey team allowed fans to bring clothes in exchange for tickets. The Hudson Motor Car Company had some of their workers cut out fabric for youth shirts.

The parishes of the Archdiocese of Detroit collected surplus crops from neighboring farms and distributed them throughout the city. Some landlords allowed many to stay rent free. Clark Park in central Detroit became a tent city for homeless citizens. Private individuals and the National Guard donated tents. Neighbors who initially opposed the encampment ended up donating food and organizing games for the children. The women organized sewing circles to make clothes. The children were able to use the park playgrounds. This freed the men to look for work.

The negative statistics were staggering. The U.S. Census Bureau declared that Detroit was the hardest hit of the twenty largest cities in the United States. The total unemployed in January 1931 was almost 250,000. Detroit was followed by Cleveland, Chicago, Buffalo, and Philadelphia.

Unfortunately, radical groups also got involved. In March of 1932, what became known as the "Ford Hunger March" was organized by

John Schmies, a Communist candidate for mayor of Detroit. Three thousand people marched from Detroit to Dearborn (a suburb of Detroit) asking for full union recognition, full employment at the Ford Motor Company, and a six-hour workday with no reduction in wages. When Dearborn police attempted to stop the march at their boundary line, a riot ensued. It resulted in four marchers being killed and hundreds being injured. About fifteen thousand marched in the funeral procession, and thirty thousand gathered near the graves and played the Communist workers' anthem, "The International." This was the song played at funeral marches after the Russian Revolution.

Tax delinquencies further exacerbated the situation, as they meant fewer tax revenues to help people. The salaries of city employees and city welfare payments had to be sharply reduced.

On February 14, 1933, Governor Comstock declared a bank holiday in Michigan. The unemployed could not pay their mortgages and people did not have money to save, so the banks were taking in very little money. Their reserves were a fraction of what they should have been. A run on banks would have been devastating. The two largest Detroit banks, Guardian and First National, were in deep trouble. Only small independent banks were staying solvent. After his inauguration in March, President Franklin Delano Roosevelt declared a national bank holiday. All banks were closed. He realized that if banks failed and if there was a run on banks, the nation's money supply would be ruined. On March 21 all solvent Detroit banks were reopened, but Detroit's two largest were liquidated. Two new banks were founded: Manufacturers Bank and the National Bank of Detroit.

Another step by Roosevelt served to boost the economy, and some say people's spirits (no pun intended). Under the Twenty-first Amendment, Prohibition was repealed and each state could decide whether to allow alcohol to be manufactured and sold again. Michigan was one of the first states to approve the manufacture and sale of alcohol. "Happy days were here again."

Other innovative measures were tried to alleviate the adverse effects of the Depression. Because there was a lack of money, the Detroit City Council issued "scrip money" to pay its employees. It was legal tender for spending in the city. The State of Michigan lacked funds to continue some services, and the state legislature passed the first Michigan sales tax.

Many of the New Deal programs did not work, but one that was extremely beneficial and successful in Michigan was the Civilian Conservation Corps (CCC). Bill O'Slattery joined this federal program and served for two summers during college. Young men, ages eighteen to twenty-five, could volunteer for this program. They lived in camps that were run by military men, mostly reserve officers. Age exceptions were made for World War I veterans. The corpsmen were paid $30 per month with $22 to $25 going to their families. This was a decent wage at this time, especially with the deflation that was haunting the economy. The first corpsmen were enrolled on April 10, 1933.

By the fall of 1934 there were sixty-one camps in Michigan with a total of 11,725 men. They wore blue denim uniforms and were initially referred to derogatorily as "wood lice." During the day, the men worked with the U.S. Forest Service or the Michigan Emergency/Conservation Works. At night they were under the control of military officers.

In the very first year in Michigan, they had planted 28 million trees and cleared 2,491 miles of trails for trucks. During their existence, they reduced fire hazards, reduced losses from tree diseases, built 13 lookout houses, built 14 lookout towers, built 4,000 fire towers, strung 75,000 miles of telephone wire, built 132,000 miles of road, fought fires, made dikes to stop flooding, and planted 1.8 billion trees. The men would work eight-hour days, and night school was provided. The program provided a partially trained group of young men who would help defeat fascism in Europe and Asia. And it also provided a group of young men who were ready to create the "arsenal of democracy." Another positive outcome was that prisoners were able to apply and many were accepted. This had a significant effect on their rehabilitation.

When Prohibition ended, the cult of lawlessness declined. Local gangs were broken up and many members were behind bars.

Some people turned to religion in the 1930s and many revivalist religions sprung up. Billy Sunday led some of these revival movements in Detroit.

Sports were also important in order to provide a diversion for the depressing times. Many called Detroit the City of Champions. In 1935, the Detroit Tigers won the World Series against the Chicago Cubs, the Detroit Lions won the National Football League Championship, and the Detroit Red Wings won the Stanley Cup. Gar Wood was racing his boats on the Detroit River and gaining national acclaim, Eddie "The Midnight Express" Tolan was already an Olympic winner, and Joe Louis, "The Brown Bomber," was on his way to becoming heavyweight champion. Detroit had become the adopted city for Joe Louis. He would become champion in 1937. He brought tremendous hope and pride to Detroiters of every nationality and race.

By the late 1930s, storm clouds were forming in Europe. Hitler's armies were beginning to invade many parts of Europe. As Europe became embroiled in war, the United States geared up to build tanks, trucks, and planes to fight it. By 1939 factories were hiring again and many people were seeing that war was inevitable. As was mentioned before, Detroit would become a huge part of the "arsenal of democracy." It was the bravery of the men and women who fought in the war that was mainly responsible for victory, but it was also the people in the manufacturing cities like Detroit that allowed them to carry out their mission. Bobbie Arquette would land in Normandy on D-Day and would fight across Europe and eventually be involved in the Battle of the Bulge. He would become a highly decorated soldier. When the United States entered the war, Bill O'Slattery had become an engineer and played a significant role in the making of military goods.

The Great Depression would end. Factories would hire the unemployed men, and for the first time, women would enter the workforce in masses. When the war began, millions of men and women volunteered to keep the world free.

The following was written by *The Detroit News*: "Detroit had suffered, struggled and survived the Great Depression with ingenuity, generosity, pride and grit."

Chapter 10

"You are the best waitress I have ever had."

The school year was one of achievement and happiness for Phyllis Arquette. It was not so much the subjects she loved, but the social dynamics of administrators, teachers, staff, and students. She was able to relate to the teachers as if she was one of them. Because of her natural social and political skills, she was able to establish friendships with her teachers that would last beyond school. Some would say she was a "teacher's pet"; yet, the other students never resented this, as it helped them form a bridge between students, teachers, and other staff. One of those was the principal of the school, Mr. McNally.

The activities of children in 1929 were significantly different than those of today. There were very few organized sports outside of the school. Children made up their own games and were only limited by their imaginations. Sports were played in the streets, vacant lots, and parks without adult supervision. It was a punishment to be made to stay inside, not a punishment to be made to go outside as it is today.

Phyllis was voted president of her class, as she would be every year until she graduated from high school. She made contributions to her school field hockey team and tennis squad because of her grit and leadership skills. She tried to join every activity she could. She organized school programs, joined the chorus, and was a skilled debater.

She became a leader in most of these activities. Parents loved coming to these programs.

Her father continued to have a difficult time adjusting to the death of his beloved wife. Like most widowers of the time, he started looking for another wife. He had to find someone to run the household so that he could again concentrate on his work. The family income was limited because of his many months of grief and mourning. At the end of 1929 he met a woman named Edith. After a short courtship, they were married in the spring of 1930. She was a large woman who had one child, Harriet. Edith doted over her daughter and the two were extremely close. William admired her cooking and housekeeping skills. When she entered the Arquette family, there was immediate tension. Edith would favor her own daughter and seemed to have few positive feelings for her stepchildren. Doris was particularly adverse to the new situation and worked even harder to graduate from high school early and escape. Doris and Phyllis continued to band together to help themselves and their two younger brothers.

At the end of 1930, the Arquette family consisted of William, Edith, Doris, Harriet, Phyllis, Bobbie, and Johnny. During that year, the home situation became difficult, if not a nightmare, for the Arquette siblings. William began working long hours again. He was able to keep a job throughout the Depression. Edith was at home with the children. Doris and Edith did not like each other from the start, and as the year went by, an enmity developed. Although a very pretty, petite, kindhearted young lady, Edith would tell Doris she was "not pretty" and not "as smart" as her older sister, Tulah, or younger sister, Phyllis. Soon Doris would seek a part-time job, do chores for other families, and study during her free hours. She knew that Edith treated Phyllis differently and was sure that Phyllis could protect the younger brothers.

Edith lavished her love and attention on Harriet and gave her extra food and material things. She did not want to raise the younger boys and was not kind to them. William was not home enough to adequately appraise the situation, and Phyllis did not want to tell him for fear her stepmother would take it out on her brothers.

Phyllis had developed the skills to get people on her side. She used flattery, good deeds, plenty of smiles, and other devices to convince Edith to leave the boys alone. If a person was not particularly attractive, she could convince them they were pleasing to look at. If a person was overweight, she was able to convince them they were not. If a person was not too smart, she could convince them they were smart. She used these skills to manipulate Edith and protect her brothers. She was becoming their surrogate mother. She usually had to cook for them, wash and iron their clothes, get them ready for school, and do all the other duties of a mother. Phyllis was able to convince Edith to allow the boys to share her bedroom. She did this by convincing her that Harriet should have a larger bedroom. In this way, Phyllis could further protect her brothers, help them with their homework, and make sure they got to bed on time.

When Edith was mean to the two boys, Phyllis immediately intervened. She planned her day so that the boys were rarely alone with their stepmother. There were times when she got home and the boys were crying and withdrawn, but they would never talk about it. At only thirteen, Phyllis was raising her first family.

The people skills she learned at this time would be helpful the rest of Phyllis's life. She was always free with compliments. Every waitress she met was the "best waitress she had ever had."

Chapter 11

The household of Raymond and Anne O'Slattery was barely holding together. Raymond was able to find less and less work. He would be away from home for days at a time now. Anne begged him to stop. He would always promise to stop drinking, but the disease would kick in and he would be off on another bender. She was afraid she would be called some night and he would be dead. Anne continued to earn money by ironing, cleaning houses, babysitting, and any other job she could get. But it was the Depression, and people had less and less money to pay workers outside of the home. She was worried that she could not help her son and that he would have to drop out of school to help the family financially. Somehow, she was able to keep things going.

On February 9, 1930, Bill came home from school and found his father playing the piano. He was sober. The two began to talk. There was excitement in his father's eyes. In moments like this, Bill always hoped that his father had stopped drinking forever.

"Bill, I need you to help me with something. As you know, my cousin Jim is a great prizefighter. He has asked me to go with him to Buffalo, New York, and help him with the finances. We need the money." His "cousin" was called Irish Jimmy Slattery and was fighting for the light heavyweight championship of the world. Raymond

O'Slattery claimed his "cousin" had dropped the first part of his name to make things easier. He was a gifted fighter. He sometimes visited Detroit in order to go to its "blind pigs." Raymond would join him.

"I need you to help me with the details and I know you would be a great help." This was all true, but his father really needed him to help him stay sober. He thought the presence of his young son would give him the strength to not drink.

Bill replied, "Sure thing. But I need to tell Mom first, and what about school? I guess I could bring my books to study on the train."

"I've already talked to your mother and she says it is okay. Just leave her a note. Tell her we will be back in a few days." Raymond lied about this.

They packed enough of their clothes and were off to the train station. Bill had a bad feeling, but he still had the naïveté of youth and loved and still trusted his father.

When Anne returned from her jobs of the day, she read the note. She was furious. She knew that her husband was putting her son in potential danger. The fight world had always been somewhat shady, with many of the underground criminals involved. She also knew about how "crazy" Raymond's "cousin" could be. But it was too late. They were off and she could only pray they would return safely. She walked out of the house to the nearby Catholic Church and stayed there until after dark. Tears streamed down her face as she realized her husband must be told to move out of the house and not return until he had stopped drinking and could hold a steady job.

Raymond always told young Bill that Irish Jimmy was his cousin, but no one was ever able to verify this. Many thought they were somehow related, but no one actually knew how. Nevertheless, Raymond and Jimmy often got together and were good friends.

By 1930, Irish Jimmy had fought many of the great boxers of the day. He fought "Slapsie" Maxie Rosenbloom, one of the greatest fighters of all time, five times and beat him four times. Their fifth fight was the only one that Irish Jimmy had lost. He had boxed Harry Greb, Tommy

Burns, Jack Delaney, Young Stribling, and Tommy Loughran, all great fighters. Irish Jimmy won the National Association Light Heavyweight crown in August 1927 by beating Maxie Rosenbloom in a ten-round decision. He defended his crown in December of the same year against Tommy Loghran in New York City and fought what some say was one of the greatest fights of all time. Unfortunately, he lost a fifteen-round decision. He took almost two years off and made a comeback in 1929. He beat Maxie Rosenbloom two times that year and won by knockout over James J. Braddock. He had earned another shot at the crown. The fight was scheduled for February 10, 1930, in Buffalo, New York, against a tough, grizzly veteran of the ring, Lou Scozza. Raymond and son Bill were on their way to Buffalo to "help out" at this fight.

Raymond had decided it was important to see this fight, as his cousin's long career was nearing an end. He also thought it was a good thing for Bill to see Irish Jimmy fight for the crown before he retired. He was willing to risk the consequences. His judgment was impaired by nearly a decade of hard drinking. Bill thought it was important to help his father. He still admired him and felt it was just a matter of time until he would be the father of his younger years.

They slept on the train and arrived in Buffalo on February 9. They took a bus to the hotel. When they got there, there was total bedlam. There were hundreds of people drinking and hanging out. They wanted to get a glimpse of the flamboyant Irish Jimmy. Irish Jimmy was one of the all-time characters in boxing history. He loved people and loved having them around him. People loved to be part of his entourage. He seemed to thrive on constant commotion and, unfortunately, constant partying. His life was totally frenetic. When he had a big fight, hundreds would show up and become a part of the party. He paid for it all. He wanted his "cousin" Raymond to organize the finances. Relatives, friends, business acquaintances, women admirers (today we would call them groupies), reporters, and those who simply were lucky enough to be close by became part of the party. Slattery made lots of money during his career but spent it as fast as he made it.

Irish Jimmy was a tall, thin, dark-haired, handsome Irishman. He was slim but very muscular and had the air of a swashbuckling cavalier. If he had lived in the mass media era, he would have been a multimillion-dollar media darling. But he also had the disease that was haunting his cousin. He fought some of his fights while being intoxicated. Some say that he would have been the greatest fighter of all time if he had taken better care of himself. There are few that would deny that alcohol abuse cut short his career. The following is from an article from the newspaper *The Buffalonian*, written by Ed Dunn.

> He came out of Buffalo's old First Ward, starting as a long rangy kid in the Broadway auditorium, to become one of the smoothest, most efficient fighting machines in the world. The first pair of green trunks he ever wore in the ring was made by his mother; the bathrobe slung carelessly over his broad young shoulders was borrowed. He fought his first professional fight for $40.00. Yet in a few swift years, Irish Jimmy's murderous left had clouted him straight to Madison Square Garden, where he eventually became light heavyweight champion of the world and heavyweight contender. In his heyday he was like the hero of some ancient Irish fable—a ring wise, black haired Irish imp who carried "man made lightning" in his gloves
>
> He fought over a hundred fights from 1924 through 1930. Those five plus years only served to grease the skids for his roller coaster ride through life. He once hailed a cab on Eighth Avenue in Buffalo and rode it nearly four hundred miles to the Adirondacks.
>
> The vanishing act was one of his pet tricks. He would drop out of sight regardless of the circumstances. His manager, Red Carrington, once lined up a big fight for him only to discover he had disappeared from sight. After five days he was arrested by the police in Elkhart,

Indiana for vagrancy. Another time he said he was going out to buy a hat. He was gone a half a week before he came back without a hat.

Once, Irish Jimmy turned up missing in Venice, Italy. His companions were getting ready to have the canals dragged when they found him at 4:00 AM, floating aimlessly around in an appropriated gondola. Anyone could put the "bite" on him. That was another of his weaknesses. That staunch heart of his was brimming with too much kindness. A buck? Sure. A fin? Sure. Fifty? Hell yes! He made more than that in a second. So the gang hung on. They used his cars, his liquor, his money and used him for all he was worth. Once a delegation of 28 hometown pals dropped into his New York hotel after a fight. They had spent all their money. How were they going to get home? Irish Jimmy snapped his fingers, "Nothing to it," he said, and ordered 29 Pullman berths for Buffalo.

What caused his rapid downfall as a fighter, as meteoric as his rise to fame? Maybe the fame was too much too soon. Maybe it was a case of "too many parties and too many pals." One guess is as good as another. Jimmy himself had the answer to the question. He once said he'd give up fighting in a minute if he could play the piano. However, he never learned to play anything but the harmonica. Minutes before his first 15 round fight he was found stretched out on a rubbing table trying to play the harmonica with gloved hands.

But for a fighter who preferred music to mayhem, he made and lost a tidy fortune. In a career of 126 fights he earned and flung away $438,000. He could have been heavyweight champion of the world according to most sports experts who saw him in action in his prime.

Gentleman Jim Corbett made it a point to see all of his fights. According to sports writers, Jim Corbett saw his own greatness mirrored in the lean Irishman. Gene Tunney called him the greatest natural boxer of those times.

Slattery boxed frequently with Tunney when the latter was getting in shape for his second Dempsey fight. During one furious session, Irish Jimmy sent Tunney sprawling through the ropes. Newspaper stories said Tunney "slipped," but Slattery's followers have always claimed that it was a clean punch that nearly knocked the heavyweight champ out.

Irish Jimmy fought his last professional fight on August 22, 1932, in Offerman Stadium. He was knocked out in the second round by Charley Belanger, Canadian light heavyweight champion.

His overall ring record would be 109 wins, 14 losses, 2 no decisions and one draw; an amazing amount of fights for the brief time he fought.

Raymond and Bill joined the entourage. Young Bill looked like he was in his early twenties and was constantly offered "bathtub gin," which flowed freely. He always refused, but watched sadly as his father did not. He stayed by his father's side and protected him. He looked like a young fighter and people did not fool with him. His father partied for three days.

In Detroit, Anne O'Slattery was worried beyond belief and was even madder. She tried to call Buffalo but got no results. She called the police, but she was told that no laws had been broken and they did not have jurisdiction across state lines. She got a hold of Raymond's other "cousin," Johnny. He said he would drive to Buffalo and do what he could do. He did this and found the party. He called Anne and told her that both husband and son were safe. He then joined the party and never called again.

People who saw the fight with Lou Scozza and reporters who wrote about it said it was one of the greatest fights they had ever seen. Buffalo's Broadway Stadium was packed to the rafters. There was green everywhere and alcohol everywhere. It was fifteen rounds of constant action. Slattery was the skilled, slick craftsman and Scozza was the brawler who could absorb tremendous punishment with the hopes of landing one haymaker. The crowd was delirious for the entire fight. Irish Jimmy hit Scozza five shots for every one he received. Scozza kept coming at him and Irish Jimmy kept moving and jabbing, throwing left hooks and an occasional straight right. It was like an Ali-Frazier fight of later years. Scozza had a few openings, but Irish Jimmy was able to weave and bob just in time to make the monster punches miss. Scozza was covered with blood when the fight ended. The decision was unanimous for Irish Jimmy Slattery. The auditorium erupted in euphoria. Most say it was his greatest fight. His entourage was ready for a day or two of partying.

After the fight, Jimmy returned to the hotel, where the celebration had begun. Police looked the other way as the liquor flowed everywhere. In the front lobby cousin Raymond was playing the piano. He was very intoxicated and Irish Jimmy knew he was in no shape to handle any of the income from the fight.

One of the men asked Raymond how he played those songs without any written music. He just smiled and said the music was in his head. Jimmy thought about how he had always wanted to play the piano.

Raymond got up and hugged his cousin as he approached. "Way to go, cuz. Best fight I ever saw. Proud to be your cousin," he said to Jimmy.

"Thanks, Raymond. Haven't seen you in a while. Is all okay? Who is that young man with you? He reminds me of me when I was starting my fight career when I was twenty," Jimmy replied.

"I'm fine. This is my son, Bill, and he is only fourteen."

"You could be a fighter with your stature," he said to Bill.

"Well, I love sports—football mostly—but my mother would not look too favorably on a life in boxing," he answered.

"Work hard at that football then, and Raymond, lay off the booze, okay?" he advised as he walked away.

Raymond O'Slattery drank all night. Bill had to carry him back to the train station and get him out of town as soon as he could. They returned home the next afternoon. They met Anne at the door and she was sickened by how bad her husband looked.

"That's enough, Raymond. I want you out immediately. Do you know the danger you put your son in? Get your stuff and get out of the house. Come back when you have stopped drinking," she was yelling through her tears.

Raymond O'Slattery left with a few dollars in his pocket and one suitcase. He slept in the street for the next few days. He had hit rock bottom.

Chapter 12

As has been pointed out, Mackenzie High School started as an intermediate school. The plan was to add a new class each winter and fall and eventually phase out the middle grades. This initial distribution enabled a relatively small number of students to be very close and very loyal to a school. They felt like pioneers. Even though Bill O'Slattery and Phyllis Arquette were not in the same graduating class, because of this unique beginning, they were able to interact constantly. They were two years separated in age; yet, they were only a half year apart in school. Phyllis had started school at four. They were both leaders of their classes and both wanted to get involved in as many activities as they could. They also shared the need to make their school their family. The school also provided a unique opportunity to interact with faculty as part of the family and the opportunity to socialize with a wide variety of students.

Phyllis and Bill were often elected as class officers, student council members, editors of yearbooks, participants in class plays, and other such activities. These activities literally forced Bill and Phyllis to get to know each other and respect each other. In addition, sports immediately became a major part of the school and all got involved in one way or another. Since Bill had become the star football player, the entire school wanted to be his friend, and many girls wanted to be his girlfriend. Even though she would never admit it, Phyllis had wanted this since the encounter at Belle Isle. The friendships and memories from Mackenzie High School would last all their lives. The "Camelot" years at Mackenzie would be one of the only things she would remember when she developed Alzheimer's disease much later in her life.

When they first ran into each other at Mackenzie, they immediately remembered their first encounter. They developed a relationship in which they would kid each other constantly. Bill called Phyllis "Frenchy" Arquette and Phyllis called Bill "O'Slats." It was a good relationship for Bill, because some of the students put him on a pedestal. Phyllis was able to keep Bill from getting "too big a head." They were both very popular. In their yearbooks they were often voted the most popular boy or girl.

They became extremely good friends. They were quite a contrast. Phyllis was less than five feet tall and still less than one hundred pounds with blonde curly hair. Bill was six feet tall and about 180 pounds with dark hair. They were able to talk to each other better than if they had been involved in any kind of romance. They talked about their home situations and these conversations served as therapy for them. They both helped each other to achieve, and who knows what would have happened if they had not become a team? If there is fate, this was a friendship that was meant to be.

They admitted late in their lives that they had "crushes" on each other starting when they went to Mackenzie, but at this time they would have never admitted it. Their constant kidding, constant laughing when they were together, and continuous shoving and poking each other in the school hallways were signs to their friends that there would be a future romance.

Bill O'Slattery, the all-*A* student and football star, had one girlfriend the entire time he was in high school. Her name was Natalie Smith, the statuesque bathing beauty he first noticed at the small beach at Belle Isle. She was a tall blonde girl of German ethnicity. Bill's mother always liked Natalie and hoped they would get married someday.

She would constantly ask Billie to ask her over for dinner. When she came, there was always a special dinner. Phyllis, of course, was aware of this romance. She kidded Bill about the tall, empty-headed blonde girl. Actually, Natalie was quite intelligent, but Phyllis would never acknowledge this.

"You just like the way she looks and like her long legs," Phyllis would chide Bill. It was he who started the long-leg thing, as he always would say how he loved girls with long, thin legs.

In typing class, Natalie would leave messages on the typewriter Bill used. Phyllis became aware of this and sometimes added things. It would go from a "Hi, Bill, miss you" to "Hi, Bill, miss u, and your bulging muscles and wonderful dark hair and dreamy eyes." Bill was never aware of this until after high school and Phyllis told him. Despite his outward appearance of maturity, Bill could be naïve and easily tricked.

In a movie of 2002 entitled *Divine Secrets of the YaYa Sisterhood*, there was a group of girls that secretly met and continued to meet throughout their lives. Phyllis and three of her new friends formed such a group. The four girls would stick together throughout high school and for the remainder of their lives.

The first to become her friend was Lucille Dodd. The school had a newspaper that carried features on the students' activities. The newspaper wrote a semi-gossip column that featured its students. The following article was about Lucille.

> Brown eyes, titian hair, five feet six inches of feminine loveliness, topped by a charming personality and magnetic smile are what make Lucille Dodd one of the most popular girls in the school. Lucille, who was voted one of the prettiest girls in her class, is of Scotch-Irish extraction with the Irish predominating, in spite of her partiality toward red berets. She has not missed a school dance in five years and has a preference for fellows who drink tea.

She and Phyllis made quite a contrast as they walked the halls of Mackenzie High School. Lucille was at least seven inches taller than Phyllis. Lucille was the prom queen type, and Phyllis was the little spitfire who was very cute but was never going to fit the mold of a prom queen.

The third girl was Dorothy Riley. She was an excellent athlete and was proud of it despite the fact that girl athletes were not as admired as they would be later in our history. She was a superb field hockey player and also excelled in tennis. Field hockey was the featured girls' sport at that time, and rivaled the boys' sports for popularity. Dorothy had a round face with big dimples. She was about five feet three inches and more muscular than her new friends. She seemed to be the medium between the other two. So, there were the petite Phyllis, the tall, thin Lucille, and the more-athletic Dorothy.

The fourth girl was Murielle Allen. She was a quiet but extremely nice girl who was liked by everyone. She was a very good student who loved to participate in as many school activities as she could. She had dark hair and eyes and was very pretty.

The "sisterhood" met before and after school, arranged classes together, and tried to be in the same extracurricular activities. Their "secret society" was to be an important part of their lives from eighth grade through high school and, as mentioned, all of their adult lives. It was another part of the "Camelot" years at Mackenzie. They could escape in their own little world and be somewhat insulated from the Depression that surrounded them.

Other close friendships started during these school years, and they would be part of Phyllis's and Bill's lives for years and years to come. A large number of the first students at Mackenzie were talented and destined for success. Like Phyllis and Bill, these young people quickly realized how important this school would be in insulating them from the troubles of the world.

Boyd Simon, who was in the same class as Phyllis, was a gifted writer. They would work together as editors of the school newspaper and most other important student publications. These frequent publications were further examples of the unique environment created by this new school. Boyd's goal was to become a journalist, and he realized his dream. He worked for over three decades as a journalist for *The Detroit News*. He was lively, energetic, intelligent, and inquisitive about things happening in Mackenzie High School, Detroit, and the country.

Oliver "Kit" Karson was a charismatic, highly motivated young man who would be one of the leaders in Bill's class. It was either Kit or Bill who would be class president. He was a fantastic debater and an orator, who won numerous contests within the school and against other schools. He had thick blonde hair and was a decorated soldier in World War II. He would enjoy a very successful career in real estate. He would eventually move to Florida and build a golf course housing development, one of the first of its kind. His nickname, "Kit," was after the famous guide who helped tame the West. This became the name he used all his life.

John Pierce had red hair and freckles. He was very extroverted and had the type of personality that made everyone like him. He was often vice president in Bill's class of '34. He and Dorothy were high school sweethearts who would marry after graduation.

Doris Krause was a tall, effervescent, beautiful girl in Bill's class. A stranger visiting the school would easily mistake her as a member of the faculty, as she had a regal bearing that made her seem older. Initially, people would think that she was somewhat of a snob, but they would quickly learn that she was not. She was always available to help anyone who asked for it. Her family owned a successful real estate business that was able to survive the economic downturn. She loved new clothes and updated styles and was one of the few girls who had enough money to keep up with the newest fashion. Kit Karson was infatuated with her the first time he saw her. They would become sweethearts and also get married after school. They were partners in their successful real estate business.

The last great friend to join the group was a big German lad named Karl Brummel. He was star offensive and defensive guard on the football team. According to newspapers, he and Bill O'Slattery speared headed the best line in the city of Detroit. He was a fun-loving young man with a kind nature. However, he was also one of those boys who had a different personality on a football field. He had a very competitive "meanness" that would come out on the gridiron. When the going got tough, he became known for throwing his leather helmet to the sideline and challenging the other team. The fans would go delirious when this happened, and the players would be electrified. It seemed to always work and bring home another victory. Bill was usually a methodical, businesslike player who rarely showed his emotions. But when Karl threw off his helmet, even Bill shifted into another gear. He and Bill would start screaming at each other and at their teammates. It was one of those things that made their football team special to the entire school.

These amazing young people, in the setting of the new Mackenzie High School, formed a bond that inspired all of them to future success. And, as important, the school environment became a special place for all of them. They would talk about Mackenzie every time they got together in later years.

Chapter 13

Detroit was not fun in the summer of 1930. The trips to such places as Bob-Lo, the Vernors Factory, and Belle Isle had slowed down. One of the exceptions was a visit to Briggs Stadium (later to be called Tiger Stadium) to watch a Tigers game, which was still very affordable. Briggs Stadium was an entirely closed-in ballpark built on the corner of Michigan and Trummel Avenues. It was easily accessible by streetcar or bus and it still only cost a quarter to sit in the bleachers and cheer for the beloved Tigers. The first impression on entering the stadium was the beautiful bright green grass of the infield and outfield.

In August, the Mackenzie clique decided to go to a ball game. Bill, Natalie, Phyllis, Lucille, Dorothy, Murielle, Johnny, Kit, Doris, Karl, and Boyd all met at the same bus stop on Michigan Avenue in eager anticipation of a fun Sunday joking with each other and watching the Tigers. They arrived at the game and all purchased their bleachers seats. The bleachers were the most fun because you could sit anywhere you wanted and never had to worry about the poles that blocked the perfect view of some of the reserved seats. The seats had been built to be as close to the field as possible, so there was a significant grade as fans walked up to their seats. If you had one of the reserved seats, you felt like you were on the field itself. The bleachers in center field were different. They were over 440 feet from home plate and sprawled out, thus creating a "party"-type atmosphere. Briggs Stadium actually had a flagpole in center field that was on the field. This atmosphere is what the Mackenzie crew loved. In the bleachers, fans were able to yell and scream and free themselves of their inhibitions. Part of the fun of the games was to buy the inexpensive hot dogs with plenty of yellow mustard, buttered popcorn, salted peanuts, Cracker Jack, Best Buy potato chips, ice cream bars, Vernors, red pop, and all the other things that people now say are not good for you.

Bill and Natalie sat together, with Natalie flirting with Bill and trying to hold his hand and sit as close to him as possible. Johnny and Dorothy sat together, talking constantly. Of all the friends, Dorothy liked baseball the most. Being a gifted athlete, she probably would have made a great fast-pitch softball player in a later era. Athletic girls were called tomboys at that time and not always encouraged to participate in sports. Kit wanted to sit next to Doris, but was too bashful. He put Doris on a pedestal and was worried this beautiful girl would not be receptive. He sat next to Boyd and spent most of the game talking about economics and politics. The four "Ya-Ya" sisters sat next to each other. Phyllis was the closest to Bill, and she used every opportunity to tease Bill and Natalie. Karl sat at one end, not saying much but thoroughly enjoying the game and happy that he was part of the crowd. They all enjoyed this beautiful day and the escape it provided. When they returned home, they were reminded of the times.

Home life was becoming more and more difficult for the Arquette siblings still living at home. Doris had graduated from business school in the spring and had moved out of the house. She returned home at times to help Phyllis as much as she could, but her stepmother was still so mean to her that it was becoming more and more unbearable to do this. She was still confident her sister could handle things. Because of the economic situation, William Arquette worked longer and longer hours, and he was unable to see the unhappiness his children experienced.

Phyllis continued to protect and act as surrogate mother to her two younger brothers. She never left them alone unless William was there. She had an exterior personality that was effervescent and extroverted; yet, inwardly she still suffered tremendously because of the death of her mother. She and her mother had been good friends and she missed her more each day. Phyllis continued to develop a side that most people did not see. She knew that the only way to survive and protect her younger brothers was to learn how to manipulate and control her stepmother.

Phyllis was also developing a phobia that would last all her life. She developed a deadly fear of cats. Her stepmother loved the longhair species of cats and brought several of these cats into the Arquette home. These cats would climb high on furniture and jump on the heads of Phyllis and her brothers. The cats would cling to their hair and scratch them. This was becoming torturous to her and affected her sleep. She asked Edith to get rid of the cats, but she thought it was funny and did nothing. This phobia became more and more severe and life at home was becoming a living hell; however, she knew she had to put up with it in order to protect her brothers. She had to find ways to not let Edith know how much she feared these cats, because it seemed to give her some sort of enjoyment. She also had to convince Edith that she liked her and that she was happy. She also did not want to let her father know what was happening out of fear of reprisals.

She was allowed to take the boys on trips. Detroit was still safe for a young teenage girl taking care of her little brothers. One of the places she loved to visit was the J. L. Hudson Department Store. This was the first and most famous Detroit department store in the heart of Detroit. It was a magical place for shoppers and visitors of all ages. It has an interesting history. The following is from an article from *The Detroit News* that narrates the early history and importance to Detroiters of J. L. Hudson's.

> In 1881 Joseph Lowthian Hudson, then 35, opened
> his first store in Detroit—a men's and boys' clothing

store—in the old Detroit Opera House Building on Campus Martius Street in direct competition with his former employer, C. R. Mabley. It was an exciting time for Detroit shoppers because of the fierce competition between the two retailers. They fought in the newspapers and initiated the "shouting" advertisement—full page ads set in large type. When the floor offered men and women clothes, the ads attracted shoving crowds of women in long dresses seeking bargains. The unpaved street and droppings of passing horses soiled their long dresses in the frantic crush. It was astonishing.

The store attracted much attention under the guidance of the innovative young merchant and he soon became wealthy. With splendid visions for the future, he insisted on expanding and offering more and more merchandise and services.

Hudson also dabbled in Detroit's fledgling auto industry. In 1909 Hudson, along with seven others, formed the Hudson Motor Car Company. The first Hudson came off the assembly line on July 3, 1909. The company's peak year was in 1929 when it stood third in the industry behind Ford and Chevrolet.

In 1911 Hudson opened his main store on Woodward Avenue. Some laughed, saying the new location was too far from Jefferson Avenue, [which] at that time was considered the center of downtown. Only Hudson himself believed his new store would become the heart of Detroit.

The next year, on a trip to his native England, Hudson, who had never married, died of pneumonia. His four nephews, all Webbers, took over his store and continued his exuberant customer-pleasing ideas.

On Armistice Day 1923 the J. L. Hudson Company unveiled a giant American flag on the side of the store. It was 3700 square feet with eight foot wide stripes and five and a half foot stars. The huge flag visited the U.S. Capitol in 1929 and the World's Fair in 1939 before it was retired in 1949.

The second huge flag weighed 1,600 pounds, used 2,038 yards of wool and covered seven stories of the Hudson building. The flag was 104 by 235 feet, and on its debut in 1950 required 55 men to hang it. In 1976, the nation's bicentennial, it was retired and was donated to the Smithsonian [Institution], which later gave it to the American Flag Foundation in Houston.

In 1924 Hudson's sponsored Detroit's first Thanksgiving Parade, beginning a long and beloved annual tradition. Charles Wendel, the display director at Hudson's, started the popular event after seeing festive holiday parades in Europe and Toronto. It was considered to be a benefit of working at Hudson's to be chosen to be among the parade marchers.

Downtown Hudson's would become a Detroit icon for years to come. It expanded to the suburbs and gave its stores names such as Northland and Westland. Sadly, as Detroit changed and people no longer traveled downtown as much, the original Hudson's was demolished in the 1980s.

The twelfth floor at Hudson's was dedicated to children. Toys and candy like the famous chocolate from Sanders Chocolate were everywhere.

It was a paradise for boys and girls. It had the largest collection of model trains and dolls of any store in the country. There were displays hundreds of feet long with model trains speeding by the model cities, tunnels, and landscapes that surrounded the tracks. Some boys (young and old) would stand by the displays and watch the trains for hours. Girls would go there before Christmas and pick out the doll they hoped Santa Claus would bring them. There were hundreds of different varieties of dolls. The floor had many more types of toys. Every popular toy of the time could be found there.

It was to this floor that Phyllis took Bobbie and Johnny. She found a comfortable seat and a good book and let them wander through this children's paradise. They didn't have money to buy anything, but the boys didn't care. It allowed them to dream of the toys they hoped to find under the Christmas tree or for their birthdays. After hours in this toy utopia, Phyllis took the boys to the cafeteria. The Hudson's cafeteria was also a popular destination for downtown shoppers. She had enough money for sandwiches and ice cream with Sanders hot fudge. Sanders Candy was another Detroit icon. The company made chocolate and fudge for pouring over vanilla ice cream. They called it a "hot fudge sundae." The candy became extremely popular in Detroit and was given at Christmas in children's stockings. Chocolate Easter bunnies, and, of course, Valentine's Day boxes of chocolates packaged in red heart-shaped boxes were a part of Detroit's traditions.

Phyllis and the boys thoroughly enjoyed their trip to Hudson's. They took the streetcar and bus back to their unhappy life at home.

Chapter 14

The 1931/32 school year was a resounding success for both Phyllis Arquette and Bill O'Slattery. Bill was now a sophomore and had finished his first varsity football season. They played an entire varsity schedule despite not having any seniors enrolled at Mackenzie High School. They were very competitive and won half of their games. Bill was named to the second-string All-City team, as was Karl Brummel. He starred as a center on offense and as a "roving center" on defense. He was also the captain of the team. He had received the usual *As* in all of his classes. Phyllis and Bill interacted in school plays and the student council. Most of their interaction was with their group of friends and through the constant kidding by Phyllis as they walked through the hallways of the school. School continued to be an escape from the real world and their sanctuary. It became a school atmosphere that probably was rarely duplicated anywhere else.

The school principal, Mr. McNally, truly loved his job and appreciated how this was a unique situation to be in. He was in charge of this new school with a special group of students. He was able to help mold the development of this school and to help the future lives the students, who worshipped him and looked at him as a father figure. There were very few discipline problems, which was part of his doing, as the students wanted to please him and follow the rules he was establishing as he went along. He was in the hallways before and after school and kept his office door open so that students could feel free to talk with him at any time. He and all the teachers would eat in the lunchroom with the students. They dined with a different group of students each day.

Sadly for the students, the school year had to end. Bill knew he had to work during the summer of 1932. He rarely saw his father, who continued to drink too much and was not welcomed in the house by his mother. He missed his father tremendously, but was able to suppress his hurt. His mother continued to take whatever odd jobs she could find. Bill found a job in a local hardware store. He worked for a few nickels a day, but anything would help the family and keep their home. His strength and work ethic were assets to his employer, who needed someone to do a lot of lifting and other physical labor. This was mutually beneficial, as it helped Bill to develop the muscular strength and endurance for the upcoming football year. He constantly looked forward to his junior season, as many predicted they would have a championship-caliber team even though it would be a team that would have seniors for the first time. He would carry wood, scrap metal, parts, tools, fertilizer, seed, and other such things from the warehouse to the store.

Phyllis did not need to work outside the home, as William Arquette's job was bringing in adequate money for the family. Also, she did everything she could to help Edith in the house so that she could continue to look after her brothers. Doris was working and seldom returned home. On one visit, she asked Edith why she was so mean to her, and Edith simply said she did not like her and that she was lucky to have had a roof over her head and food on the table. Phyllis was still the "apple of everyone's eye" and was able to control the family situation. She continued to not let her father know the true home situation. Donald, Marvin, and Tulah rarely visited the home and were met coldly every time they did.

Phyllis had decided that her main goal that summer was to take the free dance lessons for young people at the Fox Theater. The Fox Theater was a true Detroit treasure. Its construction was completed, and it opened in 1928. It was a testament to the optimism still prevalent in Detroit. The following is an excerpt from a *Detroit News* article entitled, "Detroit's Historic Fox Theatre," by Laurie Marzeja.

> When the opening-night curtain rose at Detroit's Fox Theatre on September 21, 1928, the audience of 5,000 invited guests came to 221 Woodward Avenue to see what had been billed as a "Temple of Amusement." They did not go home disappointed.
>
> The Theater, an awe-inspiring combination of Far Eastern, Indian and Egyptian styles, was the second largest Theater in the world. But it surpassed all others in grandeur.
>
> The lobby of this mammoth 10-story structure, which was six stories high and a half a block long, was surrounded by blood-red marble columns. Each column held its own jeweled figure representing Asiatic gods.
>
> The decorative scheme used subdued tones of gold to contrast a riot of color. Hangings in the lobby were golden damask and stage draperies with a wide silken fringe.
>
> Guests were greeted by notes from a small Moller organ situated over the entrance.
>
> The 3,600 square foot lobby was covered by the largest wool rug ever made by an American manufacturer. Weighing approximately 3,000 pounds, this carpet reached to the foot of the lobby's grand stairway that led to the mezzanine and balcony levels. There was an escalator and large passenger elevators—the only theater in Michigan so equipped.

The auditorium was 175 feet wide and 110 feet high. Large colonnades flanked the auditorium and behind these was a promenade where the patrons could stroll and view the entire theater. A tier of seats in the rear of the balcony were designed as smoking lounges and equipped with special fans to carry away the smoke.

The main ceiling of the auditorium was designed as a huge canopy, with sky lights above it, and decorated in the style of durbars of India.

One innovation in the movie theater construction was the inclusion of three-foot aisles in front of every row of seats. This allowed for the passage of patrons without making it necessary for those seated to stand.

The orchestra pit was built on a platform that could be raised and lowered by pneumatic pumps. Similar platforms built into the stage allowed for unusual effects. The theater was equipped with loudspeakers that would provide a uniform tonal quality throughout the entire theater.

The inaugural performance at the Fox opened with the playing of "The Star Spangled Banner" by the 60-musician-strong Fox Theater Grand Orchestra as they rose dramatically into view on the elevator platform.

On stage the inaugural production, "The Evolution of Transportation," depicted the progress of Detroit Indian days to the present utilizing a troupe of 32 dancing girls called "Tillerettes" and a choir of 50 voices.

This performance was followed by the showing of a Fox Movietone news reel—with sound! The feature film was "Street Angel," starring Charles Farrell and Janet Gaynor.

The Fox Theatre was designed by architect Charles Crane, a Detroiter who had once worked for Albert Kahn. Crane designed over 250 movie houses across Canada and the United States.

Credit for the magnificent interior of the Fox Theater belongs to Eve Leo, wife of pioneer film producer William Fox. Fox was the founder of the company which still bears his name—Twentieth Century Fox.

Fox, son of Hungarian immigrant parents, had a rags-to-riches life. Turned down around the turn of the century for a $3.00 raise from his $17.00 per week job as a pants presser in New York's East Side, Fox took his savings and bought a down-at-the-heels Brooklyn nickelodeon. At the height of the post-war boom 25 years later he was the ruler of a cinema kingdom, including Detroit's Fox Theater.

Phyllis loved going to this grand theater and loved the dancing lessons. She bragged about dancing on the stage of the Fox Theater all of her life. When she could remember little else in her late eighties, she still talked about dancing at the Fox. She excelled at tap dancing and became a part of many of the shows that the Fox produced. Altogether over four thousand children participated in the lessons and the young people's shows.

Bobbie and Johnny loved going with their sister to the dance lessons and shows. It got them away from their unhappy home situation, and it also gave them an opportunity to play in the magnificent theater. They would sometimes sit on the soft seats and marvel at its grandeur.

The Fox Theatre was renovated in the early twenty-first century and it is as magnificent as ever.

Chapter 15

Thanksgiving was a special day in Detroit. As has been mentioned, it was the day of the annual Hudson's Thanksgiving parade. Thousands would line up along Woodward Avenue and enjoy the parade. They would bring lunch to eat or buy food from the many vendors. Some Detroiters would sleep on the street the night before, or get there before dawn in order to get a good place to stand. Some would bring ladders to stand on so that they could see from the back rows. Within a few years, the Detroit Lions would play an annual football game. Initially, this game was always against the Green Bay Packers. The game started at twelve noon so that the fans could get back home in time for their turkey dinners. Santa Claus was always on the last float. His float would stop at Hudson's and he would get off at that time to the cheers of the crowd.

Mackenzie High School also started a tradition during the Thanksgiving break. Mackenzie and Redford High School agreed to play an annual game on the day after the holiday every year. The first Thanksgiving game in 1932 had added significance because it was the first time the Mackenzie football team played a full varsity schedule. The team had been competitive against all the high schools that they had played that year. Redford was undefeated at eight wins and zero losses, and Mackenzie had six wins and two losses.

The All-City team had been announced in *The Detroit News* on Thanksgiving Day. Bill O'Slattery had been named to the first team. Players played offense and defense at that time, so there were only eleven players named. Karl Brummel was named to the second team. They were the first players from Mackenzie named to the All-City teams. The paper described him as a great blocker, mentioning his great hikes (at that time teams used the single-wing offense, so the center had to hike the football about six yards to the tailback and still be ready to spearhead the blocking, since most plays were up the middle) and that he had the uncanny ability to know where the ball was on defense. He had a "nose for the ball" as they say in "footballese." The paper said that Bill and Karl, who played guard, helped Mackenzie have one of the best offensive lines in the city.

The game started at 1:00 PM under a gray, cold Detroit day. The first half was a bruising defensive battle. Bill O'Slattery was all over the field on defense, seemingly making every tackle. He even intercepted a pass.

The halftime speech by Coach Leahy was inspirational. He knew that Redford had the better team, but his All-City center was keeping them in the game through his stellar defensive play. Offensively, Mackenzie was no match for the much bigger Redford defensive line, but they still helped the team to get enough first downs to make the game a zero-zero tie at halftime. Coach Leahy knew that Redford would double and triple-team his captain on every play and try to beat him down physically. Another tactic, which was popular at that time, was to assign one player on defense to smash into the offensive center on each play. The strategy was to wear down the center and hope he would have several errant hikes.

The second half was brutal. Bill O'Slattery was literally beaten up, but he never complained and kept fighting back. He would not come out even when Coach Leahy sent in a substitute. Bill would send the player back to the sideline. Karl Brummel threw his helmet to the sideline in the fourth quarter, but it was not enough to rally his team to victory. The final score was Redford 14 and Mackenzie 0. Bloodied, Bill and Karl limped back to the locker room. They looked at each other and promised that things would be different the next year.

In the locker room, Coach Leahy spoke softly to the team. He told them that he was extremely proud at how hard they had fought. He reminded them they were mostly sophomores and juniors playing an experienced, senior-dominated team, and that next year the Friday after Thanksgiving would be Mackenzie's day for revenge. He praised the seniors and emphasized that they provided the leadership to have a great season and provided an example for future seniors to emulate.

Bruised, nose broken, legs hurting, Bill returned to class on Monday following the short holiday break. The season had been a success, but the team vowed not to lose a game the next year.

Bill's home life had not changed. After football, he decided to work part-time jobs and to study. He knew he would need a scholarship to go to college and renewed his goal to get an A in each of his courses. He would meet this goal. He was class president again. He and Kit Karson alternated in this role. Each would support the other every other year. In most schools class offices are mostly honorary positions, but this unique new school, with a progressive principal and staff, allowed student officers to have a say in school policy.

Phyllis was the class president again. She was such a good politician and so well liked that she ran practically unopposed. She also continued to study hard, and with her ability to get along with her teachers, she was able to get an A in every subject, even math. She was always given the benefit of the doubt when it came between a higher and a lower grade.

In the spring, Bill ran the mile in track and Phyllis played field hockey again. Bill did not have natural speed, but he worked so hard at conditioning that he became one of the best milers in the city. Phyllis was still valuable to the team, and the team looked to her for leadership—and even sometimes called her "Coach Phyllis."

So the school year of Bill O'Slattery and Phyllis Arquette played out like their other school years—total success and high achievement. They continued to be good friends, and Phyllis continued her good-natured kidding. When they were together, they talked about school and sports and avoided the bad economic times and their home situations. Bill and Natalie Smith continued to be an "item." On the surface it was the "perfect" match. However, all of their friends predicted that someday Bill and Phyllis would get together.

They did not look forward to summer vacation. For most things their family had become Mackenzie High School. Bill knew he would have to work. He also promised himself that he would get in the best shape he could for the upcoming football season. He wanted that scholarship. Phyllis knew her summer would be spent with her brothers. She regretted the idea of being around the home, but looked forward to a great summer participating in the great activities of Detroit with her younger brothers.

Both were looking forward to the 1932/1933 school year.

Chapter 16

The 1932/1933 school year began with high expectations. The 12-A class would be the first senior class to graduate from Mackenzie High School. Bill's 12-B class would graduate in May. The seniors looked at graduation with mixed feelings. It would signify an achievement, but would mean they would leave the "family" that had nurtured them. They knew how lucky they had been to be a part of this new school. Bill O'Slattery did not run for president, but Phyllis Arquette would continue her perfect record in that position. Their friendship had intensified. They talked more about their family situations, their goals in life, and the outside world. They were more aware of the horrible economy, as they were closer to being a part of it. They also talked about the war clouds that seemed to be forming throughout the world. They worked together on class activities, the student council, and school policy. Phyllis and Bill were together as much as Bill was with Natalie.

Bill threw himself into his studies and football. The team was outstanding and won its first eight games. He made first-team All-City again and was named to the Michigan All-State team. He was made the honorary captain of Detroit's All-City team. Karl Brummel made second team. It was Thanksgiving and time for the renewal of the Mackenzie-Redford football rivalry. Coach Leahy asked the players to sacrifice their trip to the Thanksgiving parade and practice instead. They willingly agreed. The team listened to the Lions game on the radio and proceeded to the practice field. Turkey dinner would come later. He asked the players to watch the amount they ate. "We want to be lean and mean," he joked to his players. The team was more than willing to do this. On the Friday after Thanksgiving, the team was ready.

Coach Leahy knew that he had a great team and knew that if they could play their best game they could beat his ex-team. He had taken a little time at each practice, starting with the summer practices, to prepare for Redford. He predicted that Redford would be overconfident and anticipated that they would do a little too much celebrating and eating on turkey day. There were no playoffs at this time, but his game became the "mythical city championship game," with bragging rights forever. On paper the teams were evenly matched, but Mackenzie had the motivation of revenge on their side. The seniors knew that they would be the first senior class to win all of its games. Bill had added motivation because college scouts would be watching and he needed that scholarship. He might have received a scholarship because of his academic record, but football would certainly separate him from other candidates.

The weather was clear, but brisk. All in all, it was a beautiful autumn day in Michigan. Most agree that autumn is the most beautiful time of the year in Michigan. The trees are a magnificent palette of colors—reds, yellows, light brown, oranges, and purples. The elm trees had not died off yet from the dreadful Dutch elm disease and were beautiful, as were the maple trees. These colorful trees made the new stadium bright and vibrant. The new bleachers could hold over two thousand fans, and they were completely packed. Fans lined the end zones several rows deep.

Natalie Smith sat in the front row with her friends. She had been there for two hours, as she wanted to see her boyfriend play his last game at Mackenzie. She had placed Bill on a pedestal as high as the

Penobscot Building. Phyllis was covering the game for the high school newspaper and was on the sidelines.

Most fans who have not played football do not appreciate the fierce collisions on each play. Each play only lasts six or seven seconds, and it is followed by about twenty seconds to get regrouped and have plays called. In 1932, football was mainly a running game with three blocking backs, a tailback, and seven linemen lined up side by side. It is the sounds of football that spectators never hear. Each play creates immense sound from the blocking, the tackling, and the grunts of the players. When the ball is hiked, the sounds intensify, with body on body, head on head, forearms smashing the body of their opponent. Football was played in the "trenches," as coaches like to say. Each play was an organized street fight. Most plays were running plays directly up the middle. There were few misdirection plays and deception. Only about 5 percent of the plays were passes. This means that the strongest, most motivated, and best-conditioned team usually won.

Coach Leahy remembered the beating his center had taken the previous year. He remembered how a player had been assigned to smash into his center, Bill O'Slattery, on every play. So he devised a method of protecting him that he practiced every day but never used in the other games that year. Immediately after hiking, Bill would take a quick step into the "A" gap. This is the gap between the center and the guard. He mixed up which side he would move to so that Redford could not anticipate where he would be. He put Karl Brummel at blocking back. He and Bill would have a signal to say which gap he would step. When the ball was hiked, Karl would smash into the Redford player as hard as he could. The strategy would work so well that two Redford players were carried off the field in the first half and they had to change their strategy. On defense, he had his line block the offensive linemen and not worry about the ball. He wanted his captain to be free to roam from sideline to sideline and be in on every tackle.

Mackenzie won the toss and elected to kick off. Coach Leahy told them to scream as they ran down the field. He wanted to start on defense the first series. The coach wanted to create an early psychological advantage, and it worked perfectly. Mackenzie controlled the first half and took a 7 to 0 lead at halftime. Bill O'Slattery was all over the field, making vicious blocks and tackles. Karl Brummel and the rest of the team were outstanding. Bill was exhausted when he left the field, but his summer conditioning would pay dividends the second half.

At halftime, Coach Leahy kept reminding his team to stay motivated and play the half as if the score was 0 to 0. He told them that Redford would be fired up to start the second half. "Undefeated," "city champs," "a memory for a lifetime" he kept telling his team. He changed his strategy for the second half, causing the Redford coaches to waste the time they had spent at halftime trying to adjust to Mackenzie's first-half strategy. Karl Brummel was put back at guard on offense, and the defensive line was told to follow its normal techniques.

Coach Leahy asked Bill if he could keep up the intensity for thirty more minutes. He was asking a lot.

Bill replied, "I could do it for sixty more minutes, Coach."

The second half began. Redford chose to receive. The Mackenzie side of the field went dead silent as Redford's best running back returned the kickoff for a touchdown. The Redford fans went wild.

Mackenzie received the next kickoff and started their methodical offense. Quickly the play reverted to the same pattern as the first half—three plays and a punt. Together the teams would punt thirty times in the game. This made the center extremely important, as an errant hike could cost his team the game. On defense, Bill O'Slattery continued to be in on almost every tackle. Each time his body got more and more beat up, and each time it took him longer to get up. But when the play started—those six seconds of fury—he somehow was ready to go.

The crowds on both sides became more and more tense. Loud cheering turned to anxious gasps. All who knew football realized that this was a brutal, epic battle being fought by sixteen-, seventeen-, and eighteen-year-olds. They seemed older. Football resembled war in so many ways. This would be the generation that would endure the Great

Depression. This would be the generation that would fight five years in World War II. They would be part of the generation that defeated the evil forces of fascism in Germany, Italy, and Japan. It would be the generation that would risk everything in the landing on the beaches of Normandy. And when that was accomplished, it would be the generation that led the fight to defeat the next evil in the world—the totalitarianism of communism. It would be a selfless generation that developed the entrepreneurial skills to make the United States the strongest economy in the history of the world. The grit shown on the faces of these young men was representative of the true spirit of America. Those who led the Revolution of 1776 would have been proud of them.

Some skeptics argue that sports should not be played to win but to just have fun. But that is not the American spirit. Those who truly understand sports know its participants should always try to win. Winning means trying to be the best parent one can be, or trying to be the best one can be on his or her job. It means doing everything possible to be self-reliant. It means trying to pull one's weight. You don't have to win every battle and challenge in life, but you have to make the *effort* to win every battle and challenge. Participation in sports teaches this important American value.

The fourth quarter continued to be a brutal defensive battle. Each young man was being pushed by their coaches to continue to fight. The conditioning of the Mackenzie players and the fact they practiced and sacrificed on Thanksgiving was beginning to pay off. The Redford players were starting to wear down. The players knew that the winner would never forget a victory today and the loser would never forget a defeat. This type of game transcends the game itself.

Time was winding down. Neither team wanted a tie. Redford had the ball on its own forty-yard line with less than a minute to go in the game. They were no more time-outs. Running plays would probably run out the clock. Redford's coach called for a pass. Of course, Coach

Leahy anticipated this and sent in a substitute to tell his captain to drop straight back as soon as the ball was hiked.

As instructed, when the ball was hiked Bill O'Slattery backpedaled as fast as he could. The Redford tailback threw a pass as far as he could down the middle of the field. Their two ends converged on the ball the same time as Bill did. O'Slattery jumped higher than he had ever jumped before and managed to catch it and cradle it in his sweat-soaked uniform. He began to run as fast as he could.

Karl Brummel was in front of him. He screamed at Bill, "Run, Bill, run! I'm with you. Run your fucking ass off."

The Redford players were caught by surprise and slightly delayed their pursuit. Two of Redford's fleetest backs started sprinting at Bill. They were twenty yards behind Bill when he crossed the fifty-yard line. They closed in on him as he crossed the twenty-yard line. Brummel made his move. He turned around and delivered one of the fiercest blocks imaginable. In a vicious crash he took out both pursuers, and Bill found a new gear as he sped across the goal line. The game was over. Mackenzie had secured its first undefeated season. Its captain had scored the winning touchdown. The Detroit newspapers had a picture of the "block" and a view of Bill O'Slattery crossing the goal line. Later in the century, he would be chosen as captain of the all-time Mackenzie football all-star team.

In the locker room after the game, Coach Leahy told his players that he had never been prouder of any group of young men in all his life.

Chapter 17

"Most popular youth lacks dance partner."

Principal McNally wanted as many extracurricular activities in his school as possible. He also wanted to start special events that would become yearly traditions. He believed a purpose of education was to develop the entire person. One of the things he started was a spring school play. They had started to have plays, but they were small. He wanted an extravaganza that would appeal to students, faculty, and parents.

The first thing he decided to do was to get one of the most popular teachers to produce the play. He thought this would get more students to participate. He was correct. He knew who to choose. Miss Hannigan was an English teacher who was the most popular teacher in the school. Miss Hannigan had graduated from college the year before the school opened and had known the students from the beginning. She looked about the same age as the seniors. She was particularly liked by the boys. Mr. McNally knew that was important to get the boys to participate. She had good organizational skills and was a hard worker, but she knew nothing about putting on a play. Therefore, she decided to let the students select the play, direct it, and do the choreography. A large number of students volunteered to participate. She knew who would be the perfect person to put in charge, and asked Phyllis Arquette to stop by her classroom after school.

"Phyllis, I need someone to help me produce the school play. I think you would be perfect for this. Mr. McNally wants this to be an annual event and knows that the first production would be critical for future endeavors," she told Phyllis after she arrived in her classroom.

"Sure, I would love to," Phyllis immediately replied.

On the way home from school, she picked up her two brothers as usual and immediately began thinking about the type of play they should have. She asked them if they minded staying with her after school while she worked on the play. Her first obligation was to take care of Bobbie and Johnny. They agreed without giving it a thought, remembering the fun they had had at the Fox Theater.

For the next several weeks, Phyllis and Miss Hannigan scoured through as many plays as they could, trying to get ideas. Nothing seemed to fit their school. So Phyllis volunteered to write a play totally from her imagination, and Miss Hannigan agreed.

She came up with an idea of a romantic comedy and spent every free moment she had writing a two-act play. She called her play *Eleanor and John*. Miss Hannigan helped her with the final draft and was very pleased with the quality of the work, especially how funny it was. Together they made plans for scenery and sets. They had an open call for casting but had a good idea who would play the leads. The lead parts went to Lucille Dodd and Boyd Simon. Kit Karson and Doris Krause were perfect for the backup roles. Natalie Smith was a rival femme fatale. At least forty students became involved with the play in some manner. Bill O'Slattery helped to make the sets.

Phyllis was like a little dictator as she yelled and screamed constant directions at the rehearsals. Miss Hannigan was always present at these rehearsals, but she let the tiny director/producer be in charge. Phyllis even wrote a part in which there were tap dancers. She taught five freshmen how to tap dance for their part in the play and choreographed a routine. The tap dance became one of the best parts of the play.

Opening night was in early May. There was a dress rehearsal the day before after school for the faculty. Almost every detail had been orchestrated by the little general. Every part of the play worked to perfection. Each student was fantastic.

Principal McNally was amazed at the production and said to Miss Hannigan, "It was like a Broadway production."

He added, "What ability that little lady has. She is very special. I wonder where life will lead her. Can she get through the gender barriers in our society? I think if she were a boy she would have a shot at being a governor or senator or whatever."

The school play was a resounding success in each of its four performances. The local newspaper gave it rave reviews and marveled at how a young high school student could write and produce such a polished, entertaining, and funny play. A tradition had started.

Mr. McNally also started senior-sponsored dances. They were a source of income, as they charged a nickel per student; but more importantly, they were an excellent way to carry out the social part of school. Twice a month in the second semester of school, they held dances in the school cafeteria. High school was so much more innocent in 1933. There were strict rules and rituals that were followed at school dances. There was a stag line where the boys would stand until they got the nerve to cross the dance floor and ask a girl to dance. They would have decorations, refreshments, and a small school band playing. The students would dress up in their best clothes. Boys, if they could afford one, would wear a suit and tie. There were always teacher and parent chaperones. They were never short of volunteers, because it was so much "good, clean fun."

At the last dance of the year, the girls at Mackenzie decided to play a trick on Bill O'Slattery. The following is an article from the student newspaper that shows the conspiracy. It shows the innocence of the time.

Most Popular Youth Lacks Dance Partner

Big Bill O'Slattery has finally met his Waterloo! O'Slats was all-city center in football and for two consecutive years has been elected the most popular boy in school—but the 12-B girls were too much for him. O'Slats strolled in the senior dance last week with a dignity befitting one of so exalted a position. He joined the stag line for a few minutes until the orchestra swung into the exotic strains of "Honestly, I Love You." O'Slats squared his mighty shoulders. Would these lowly 12-B hearts flutter when the great O'Slattery asked for a dance?

He walked over to a flimsy young thing and bowed. She said, "No." Thinking she had misunderstood him, O'Slats tried another. She wasn't dancing either, thank you. The next girl he approached was ill. So was O'Slattery by this time. He gazed back at the stag line and was met by knowing grins which seemed unnecessarily malicious to the bewildered football hero. Bill decided the lunchroom was rather warm even for a spring day.

O'Slattery doesn't like tea but he liked his present position even less. So with a final attempt to regain his faith in the young ladies, O'Slats went after some refreshments.

Natalie Smith came late to the dance because she knew about the practical joke. When she arrived, Bill finally had a dance partner.

Chapter 18

The senior year was coming to an end for Bill O'Slattery. The year had been another tremendous success. His friend Kit Karson was elected president of the class. He had received numerous awards in the Detroit Metro area for debating. Before graduation, Bill was nominated for a scholarship to attend the City College of Detroit. His mother, Anne, had done everything to pay the bills, but had no extra money. Bill had to turn down the scholarship. It covered tuition, and room and board. But Bill did not have the money to pay for books or any other expenses. The following article from the school newspaper explains what happened.

O'Slattery Gives Up C.D.C. Scholarship

William O'Slattery, former Mackenzie football star, who won the scholarship to the College of the City of Detroit offered to a member of every graduating class last May, has forfeited his claim to the honor because of financial reasons. The scholarship was transferred to Oliver Karson, president of the May class. O'Slattery gave his reasons for not taking the advantage of the free tuition. He declared that, despite the scholarship, attending City College involves other expenses such as books, activities fees, and other financial requirements which he did not feel he would be able to meet.

The loss of the scholarship is not preventing Bill from attending college, however, for he has enrolled at Lawrence Tech on a co-operative basis, working in the Briggs plant in the time he does not attend classes. He is also an outstanding candidate for the football squad at the Institute.

Catholics sometimes say, "When one door closes, another one opens." And this was the case for Bill. In fact, it was of the best things to ever happen to him. His lifelong dream of working for the automobile industry would now be launched. Lawrence Technical Institute was a college catering to the automotive engineering needs of Detroit. Bill would major in mechanical automotive engineering, but the school would specialize in courses that would prepare engineers for the automotive industry. The cooperative work program enabled students to receive valuable work experience for the automotive companies. Bill would work and attend college at the same time.

Lawrence Tech had an outstanding football program at this time. They could compete with every university in the state except for the University of Michigan, and some even said they would hold their own with UM. Bill would make all-conference his first three years, but knee injuries ended his career after his junior year.

The graduation ceremony in May 1933 was extremely important for Mackenzie. The first graduation ceremony was actually in January, but it only had a few students and these students also attended the May ceremony. The widow of David Mackenzie gave the graduation speech. Kit Karson was the valedictorian, having never received a B in school. Bill O'Slattery was the salutatorian because he had received a B in typing. All their speeches were filled with humility and optimism. Mrs. Mackenzie wanted everyone to know how her husband would have been proud of this graduating class and the excellent faculty. She concluded her remarks by saying she was sure her husband was "looking on from above." Kit Karson's speech brought the audience to its feet. He was a gifted speaker. After a few introductory remarks, Bill O'Slattery said the following.

> I would like to thank Mrs. Mackenzie for her inspiring words. I also think he is looking down on us. This school is an excellent testimony to his greatness and dedication to education. I would like to thank Mr. McNally, our fantastic principal. He has been a friend and a mentor to all of us. I speak for all the seniors at Mackenzie High School when I say that this has been the most wonderful four years that any high school student could have. Mackenzie has been a family for us. We have been prepared for the world by a magnificent group of dedicated and inspirational teachers. All of them, just like Mr. McNally, have been friends as well as teachers to us. They have provided us with knowledge, for sure, but also the life skills we need to succeed in life. We are now ready to enthusiastically begin our long difficult journey in life. We are having troubles in our economy. We will help to solve these problems. (This brought a cheer.) There will be peaks and valleys, but we will be able to handle them because of our experiences at Mackenzie. We are not afraid to work and look forward to the time when we can all pull our own weight. I want to thank Coach Leahy. He has been a second father to me. Also, Coach LaRue has been fantastic. He worked so hard and never complained about not receiving the accolades he deserved. I will always be thankful to all the fantastic students at Mackenzie, my fellow athletes, and all of the special friendships I have been lucky to

have. Finally I want to thank my parents. My mother has been my best supporter. She has always supported me and pushed me to succeed. I could not have had a more wonderful or stronger mother. Thank you, Mom. I would also like to thank my father for all of his advice as I grew up. He is ill and not able to be here today. We have all been very lucky to be students at this brand-new school. I know we will never forget our wonderful life here. Thank you for the honor of speaking to you today.

The students applauded with happiness and sadness, as they knew it was over. He was summing up the thoughts of all the graduating students.

Chapter 19

The summer of 1933 would be an exciting and challenging one for Bill O'Slattery. He worked as an intern for the Plymouth Automobile Company and worked out daily for the upcoming college football season. He continued to date Natalie Smith, but was unsure how long this would last. There was an enormous physical attraction, but more and more, he felt something significant was lacking. He wanted a woman who could understand him, could understand why he was so ambitious, and could understand his deepest needs and feelings. Natalie was fun, but their conversations were superficial and mundane. He needed more, but was not sure what that entailed. His mother continued to sing the praises of Natalie, and she continued to hint that they should someday get married.

By the summer of 1933, Bobbie and Johnny were learning to hold their own against their stepmother. They were both entering intermediate school (now called middle school). In many ways, their childhood made them tough and ready for the hard knocks of life. They still treated Phyllis more like their mother than an older sister, but they were less and less dependent on her. This would be their last summer of excursions into Detroit. Their father started to realize what was going on in his home and willingly gave Phyllis and the boys the money to get out of the house to have fun in the city.

This summer, their most frequent trips were to the Jefferson Beach Amusement Park, which was located in St. Clair Shores, a suburb of Detroit. They could take a bus directly to the park. The ride they liked the best was call the "Big Dips," later to be called the "Big Dipper." The "Big Dips" was considered the best roller coaster in southeast Michigan. Phyllis would escort them on the bus and then let them play by themselves for hours and hours.

Trips to Belle Isle were also part of this fun summer. Phyllis promised to take them to every landmark on the island. They went to the conservatory, the aquarium, the casino, the nature center, the zoo, and the swimming beach with its water slide. They liked to paddle the canoes down the canal, bicycle along the long nature trails, and sometimes just run around the vast fields. Sometimes they would bring their baseball gloves and bats and play a game of baseball with the other children. Phyllis would pack a hearty lunch, which would be enjoyed at one of the numerous picnic shelters. Like at the amusement park, Phyllis would allow the boys to take care of themselves.

The Bob-Lo boats had resumed their trips to the island, and the threesome took several trips to this wonderful place that summer. Like Doris and Phyllis a few years before, they loved to ride on the fantastic carousel and to run and slide on the huge dance hall floor. Again, part of the fun was playing during the ferry ride to and from the island.

This summer was glorious for Phyllis and the two boys.

Chapter 20

Phyllis Arquette looked forward to the last half of her senior year. She would graduate in January. She loved and still needed Mackenzie High School. It gave her enormous self-esteem and continued to be her sanctuary. Like Bill O'Slattery, she looked forward to graduation like most seniors do, but she knew that she would be very sad to leave her second family. She vowed to get involved in as many activities as she could. Bobbie was now able to take care of himself and to protect his younger brother. She knew that her role as a surrogate "mother" was coming to an end. She was proud of what she had accomplished. But like leaving high school, this would be a little sad. This threesome had become a family within a family, and she knew the bonds between them would change. For the rest of her life she never bragged about what she had done, but one could tell she was proud of it.

The year started with elections to the student council. She ran again for her homeroom representative and won without opposition. She wanted to run things and her fellow students wanted her to do it. She then decided to run for an officer's position on the council. A girl had never held this position. She did not feel she could be president of the council, so she ran for vice president. Most knew she would run things regardless of the position she held. It was simply her nature.

"If you elect me to the vice president's position, you students know that I will be able to deliver more for the students than any other candidate," she said every chance she got. The students knew she would be able to deliver on her promises. The election was a landslide victory. The following article from the school newspaper describes the results.

Arquette First Girl to Be Council Executive

The regime of male executives was finally broken when Phyllis Arquette was elected to the vice-presidency of the Student Council. After a period of three years of male mandates, the fairer sex succeeded in breaking into the exclusive circle.

Phyllis played field hockey again and was chosen by the coach to be the captain. She was like the team's quarterback during its games. Her friend Dorothy was the star of the team.

It became time to elect the president of the senior class. Again, no female had ever held this position. In fact, no one had dared run before. Her friends Dorothy, Murielle, and Lucille helped her with her campaign. They posted advertisements in the *Mackenzie Dial* and made flyers to hand out to every member of the senior class. Above all, she made speeches every chance she got. As was mentioned before, it was said, "She may be little, but she makes herself heard." Nowhere was this more evident than in this campaign. Mr. McNally again made the comment to a teacher, "If she were a man, we would be looking at the future governor of Michigan." The other candidates did not stand a chance. The *Dial* reported:

Phyllis Arquette President of the Senior Class

Shatters Long Tradition through Decisive Victory
Phyllis Arquette, who has been outstanding in her class activities since the seventh grade, won the distinction

Wednesday of being the first Mackenzie girl to attain the senior class presidency. She gained the office as a result of her victory over Boyd Simon. Phyllis swept the election by the overwhelming vote of 79 to 34.

Speeches by the five original aspirants preceded the elimination balloting. The campaign thus set in motion momentum when members of the senior class appeared wearing tags in support of the two surviving candidates, and culminated in the final election.

"I feel greatly honored to have the office bestowed upon me," said Phyllis Arquette after the election to the presidency of the class, an office she had held the past two terms. "It is a good class, and I shall do my best to make it even better."

Phyllis is a member of the National Honor Society and vice-president of the Student Council last term. She has served as president of her homeroom since seventh grade.

In the spring, Phyllis again directed and produced the school play. This time, she and Miss Hannigan found a play they could use, so she did not have to write it. Lucille was again the leading lady. Lucille was one of the most popular girls in the class and one of the most talented. The following article from the *Dial* gives a description of Lucille. It shows the innocence of the time also.

Popular Girl Graduate Indicates Preferences
Likes Tea-Drinking Youths and Bright Red Berets

Brown eyes, titian hair, five feet six inches of feminine loveliness, topped by a smile, and magnetic personality are what tend to make Grace Lucille Dodd one of the most popular girls in the senior class.

Lucille, who was voted one of the prettiest girls in the graduating class, is of Scotch-Irish extraction, with the Irish predominating, in spite of her partiality toward red berets. She has not missed a school dance in five years, and has a preference for the fellows who drink tea.

Entering Mackenzie when it opened in the eighth grade, Lucille has completed five years here. She has enjoyed the time spent in school with the excellent faculty and students which Mackenzie boasts. Lucille plans to attend business school upon graduation.

The Mackenzie 12-A, Class of 1934, had been a great one. The football team was not as good, but still competitive. Boyd Simon was valedictorian and Lucille Dodd was salutatorian. Phyllis made the honor roll again. The Detroit Board of Education gave scholarships to the recently opened City College of Detroit to one deserving student in each major public school in the city. Phyllis Arquette was a recipient of this scholarship. She was the first female to be so honored. The following letter was sent to her notifying her of this selection.

Miss Phyllis Arquette
Maple Street
Detroit, Michigan

My Dear Miss Arquette:

Upon the recommendation of your high school principal, you have been selected as the recipient of the Board of Education scholarship from Mackenzie High School for the beginning of the fall term.

The scholarship will entitle you to attend the City College of Detroit for one year without paying the usual tuition fee. You will be expected to pay the student activity fee, which amounts to $6.50 each semester. Should you not be able to accept this scholarship, will you kindly let me know at the earliest date so that we may select an alternate.

Dean,
City College of Detroit

Articles in the Detroit newspapers indicated that Phyllis Arquette had received this scholarship, described her achievements, and pointed out that she was the first woman to receive a scholarship to the City College of Detroit. Phyllis had achieved another first.

The senior year had come to an end for Phyllis and her class. She had excelled beyond others' expectations, but not her own. She knew she had extraordinary abilities and wanted so much to go to college and become the first person in the Arquette family to graduate from college. She was sad to leave Mackenzie High School but was excited and optimistic about her future. Being a woman in a man's world was of no concern to her. She had constantly held leadership positions and was competent holding them. Why should this not continue?

Phyllis had dated during high school, but she never had a steady boyfriend. She had plans for this also and knew who would be her first and, hopefully, only boyfriend.

Chapter 21

*P*hyllis Arquette walked into her first class at the City College with unbridled exuberance, optimism, and glee. She missed the days at Mackenzie, but she was now embarking on an adventure that could take her to unbounded success. She was a young woman on a mission, as they say. She decided she would major in speech. In the back of her mind she wanted politics to be her path to success. She reasoned that her past election successes could be continued outside of school. She always loved the debating tournaments she participated in and was buoyed by her success in them. She knew that her speaking skills could be transferred to politics. After all, she had never lost an election.

She excelled this first semester. Without math she was able to earn an A in every subject. She became popular with every teacher, always asking and answering questions. She would "size up" her teachers. She would play with their minds, flatter them, make them feel special. She had been approached to get involved with student government and started planning her campaign for the second semester. President of her class would be her goal. She put together a committee of friends to help her.

She arrived home with the good news about her grades and showed her father the good news as soon as he returned from work. Her father looked at them without emotion and coldly said, "They are wasting that scholarship on a girl. It should go to a boy. What are you doing, wasting their money? If you keep it, you have to move out or pay room and board."

Phyllis was devastated and livid. She wanted to hit her father as hard as she could. She had loved her father and always admired him, but her current feelings were all negative. She wanted to hit him as hard as she could. She never knew she felt this way. Thankfully, she was speechless for one of the few times in her life. She went to the kitchen, helped Edith with dinner, ate quickly, cleared the table, helped wash the dishes, and went to her room. She realized it was time to get out of the house. She had to find a job because she could not afford college on her own. She thought about her two brothers and concluded that they were old enough and strong enough to take care of themselves. Bobbie would have to be the protector now and he was able to do it. She also decided she had to tell her father about Edith. She would spare details but let him know enough to hopefully make him look out for the boys.

Raising her first little family was now over. She was proud of what she had done.

The next day she went to Doris' house, as she was the only one who could help her. Doris was now married. She and her new husband allowed Phyllis to stay with them until she was able to fend for herself. Doris worked in the office of Tuttle & Clark, an upscale department store. She was able to get Phyllis a job as a salesperson. Doris continued to be a rock in her life.

Her dreams of college were now over. She came to the realization that she would have to use her skills in other ways. She realized that she could use these gifts in a family of her own.

Phyllis found the sales job to be tedious and not enough of a challenge. She started to practice the typing, shorthand, bookkeeping, and other office skills she had learned at Mackenzie. At the time she took them, she had no idea how beneficial they would be.

Despite the bad economy, she was able to use her charm to obtain a job as a secretary with the commercial real estate firm of Johnson & Williams. She really liked her boss and loved this job, quickly becoming indispensable to the firm. She obtained power at the firm in a relatively short period of time by learning about all phases of the business. She learned about the legal aspects of real estate contracts, the financial parts of the business, the listing process, and all the other nuances of commercial real estate. Within a year she was promoted to office manager. She was able to use her charm and people skills to become friends with the clients and was able to find new clients. She would talk to people when she went out to lunch, while riding a bus or streetcar, or in any other place she could talk to people. Her boss, Mr. Johnson, talked to her about becoming a broker and she seriously considered this as a future life. There was a lot of societal pressure for young ladies to marry and have a family. And she knew this would probably be her direction. However, she would talk favorably about her job and her kindly boss for the rest of her life, even when most of her memory was erased in the last few years.

Phyllis was popular with men but more as a sister. She was so cute and looked so young that men looked at her more as a buddy than in a romantic way. Phyllis knew in her heart that there was one young man who was perfect for her. That was Bill O'Slattery, who was now successfully attending Lawrence Tech. She still had a crush on him and always thought he felt the same way. She wondered about Natalie and how that romance was going.

She and Bill would sometimes run into each other on a bus, shopping at Hudson's, or walking around the city. One day they were both eating lunch in the cafeteria at Hudson's in downtown Detroit. Bill invited her to sit with him. They resumed their good-natured kidding and talked about their days at Mackenzie. She got up the nerve to ask about Natalie and if they were still a couple. She held her breath as he said, "No."

The chemistry between the two was still there. They were still quite a contrast. Bill stood a little over six feet tall and Phyllis was still less than five feet tall. Bill outweighed her by over a hundred pounds. He had put on even more muscle since high school, as he had to gain weight for college football. He had grown a small mustache and now wore glasses all the time. Even though they were almost two years apart in age, Bill looked much older. When they stood side by side, Bill towered over her. But it did not matter. Bill would soon develop the habit of bending over slightly to make himself look shorter. Phyllis got up the nerve to suggest that they get together sometimes. Without hesitation he said, "Yes." However, he did not have time to date anyone until he graduated. Because of work, classes, and studying, he had little time for dating. Phyllis would wait.

Bill O'Slattery graduated in 1938 from Lawrence Tech with a degree in mechanical engineering. He had met his goal. He excelled in the classroom and his work assignments at The Chrysler-Plymouth Company. His father had been right. Football had helped give him a helping hand for success, and he had two bad knees to remind him. But he had transcended his football prowess in every way. He had excelled in the classroom as much as on the football field. His father attended his graduation ceremony. He was thinner and his hands shook constantly, but somehow he seemed different. This made Bill extremely happy and relieved. Even though Bill did not know it, Phyllis was also in the audience.

Bill O'Slattery met Raymond and Anne O'Slattery after the ceremony. Raymond told them that he had hit rock bottom and had now quit alcohol for the remainder of his life. He asked if he could return to the house. Anne could tell he was sincere and readily said, "Of course."

Raymond never talked about what he did after returning from the Jimmy Slattery fight. It was part of his life that he was not proud of and wanted to forget. During one conversation, Anne asked him what made him finally quit drinking. He had tremendous fear in his eyes as he kept silent.

Bill was tremendously pleased that his father had returned, and he wanted him to be part of his future life and his mother's life. Raymond once told Bill that he had seen all of his football games from high school through college, but because of his drinking, he felt it best to stay in the background and not be seen. After his return, he loved talking to his son about the two games with Redford. He gave Bill a scrapbook he had kept since his first game. As would be expected, this was immensely appreciated by his son. Anne was happy her husband was back. He was sober, and most importantly, alive.

Raymond and Anne stayed together for the rest of their lives. Raymond was able to return to work. Because of his hand tremors, he was not able to work on complicated jobs, but his knowledge enabled him to be a great electrician's helper. Anne continued to work and together they bought a beautiful little house. It was perfect for the visits of their future grandchildren. He also continued to play the piano without music. Anne became a fan of horse racing and spent some of her leisure time at the racetrack. She never wagered much, but loved to talk about her luck.

With her success on her job and pay raises, Phyllis was able to move out of Doris's home and rent a small apartment near her work.

On a beautiful summer day in 1938 underneath Kern's Clock, another Detroit icon, Bill and Phyllis accidentally ran into each other. Kern's Clock is on Woodward Avenue. Their eyes met and they knew they needed each other. They subconsciously knew many years before that their love would surface.

"Hi, Bill. How are you doing? Congratulations on your graduation. I knew you would do it," Phyllis started.

"I'm doing fine, thanks. I just started a full-time job at Plymouth. It is fantastic. How are you doing?" Bill replied.

"Well, college didn't work out. My dad said I could not live at home if I kept my scholarship. He didn't believe in girls getting scholarships. I had no money to start out on my own. I lived with Doris for a while but didn't feel right living off her and her new husband. With the economy they did not have much extra money. Anyway, I gave up my scholarship and went to work. I have been working at Johnson & Williams. It is a good job and I like it, and it pays enough for me to get my own place. Still not seeing Natalie?"

"Nope, we are history. 'Footloose and fancy free,' as they say."

Bill was usually not this spontaneous, but he thought he and Phyllis should get together before it was too late.

"Let's go out. I work Monday through Saturday most weeks, but I am free on Sundays. Let's go to Belle Isle. I love that place and I seem to remember a sassy girl I saw there one time." Phyllis had never forgotten that first encounter either. They would talk about it the rest of their lives.

"Sure, would love to. How about Sunday around one o'clock? I'll meet you here at Kern's Clock," Phyllis replied, barely hiding her glee.

"Perfect. See you this Sunday. I've been thinking about you lately. I've been wondering how the leader of Mackenzie has been doing and if we would ever get together," he said with a smile.

"And I've been wondering how the football star has been." Phyllis returned the quip. They walked away in opposite directions, both thinking something wonderful was happening.

Chapter 22

It was a beautiful fall Sunday in Detroit when Phyllis Arquette and Bill O'Slattery met under Kern's Clock.

"Hi, Phyllis. How are you? You look very nice." Bill was wearing his Mackenzie letter sweater. The huge M was quite vivid on the gray and blue jacket. Phyllis chuckled a little when she saw him. She remembered how poor Bill had been and how often he had had to wear it. But he was still proud of it.

"I'm good," Phyllis replied. She still looked like a schoolgirl. She wore a print dress with kneesocks and flats. She still could pass for a young teenager.

"Ready for Belle Isle?" Bill said as they gave each other a quick hug.

"Sure. Let's get to the nature center. I brought lunches," she replied as the streetcar came to a stop near them.

As they traveled down Woodward Avenue, they talked about their days at Mackenzie and about their current lives. Taking the streetcar was still fun for them. They both agreed that their days in high school had been magical times.

They took the ferry to Belle Isle and walked to the nature center. This center had numerous paths to walk on. Its vegetation was spectacular. It displayed all the flora and fauna of Michigan. They slowly walked along the paths, constantly talking and kidding each other. They walked for over an hour and then sat on one of the benches and ate their lunches. The leaves were starting to turn and Belle Isle was beautiful. Bill liked to point out the different types of birds. He was a lifetime bird-watcher and had just joined the Audubon Society. The days were getting shorter now and they decided they should return before dark.

"This has been so much fun. I so enjoyed being with you, Phyll. Let's do it again next Sunday and meet earlier so we have more time." He still called her "Phyll" and sometimes would call her "Frenchy Arquette."

"I would love to. We could do something different each time," she answered and quickly glanced at Bill to see his reaction to the words "each time." Bill had a grin on his face.

They returned to Kern's Clock and each took a bus home. They both felt that something special was happening. They could talk about all the things in the world as well as their past days at Mackenzie. They seemed to understand each other and especially loved being together. The romance was "officially" starting on this cool, clear Michigan fall day.

They met the next Sunday at ten o'clock. They again met at Kern's Clock. Bill was no longer wearing his "M" sweater. He would never wear it again. They decided to go to Belle Isle again, but to visit the other attractions. They talked constantly on the streetcar and the ferry ride to the island. It was another beautiful fall day in Michigan. Of the two Bill was the more serious, yet he also had a keen sense of humor that was pleasing to Phyllis.

They first visited the aquarium, enjoying the tremendous variety of aquatic life. It was America's oldest freshwater aquarium and had received numerous honors for breeding stingrays. Phyllis and Bill enjoyed watching them glide through the water. They enjoyed the electric eels and all the other types of fish indigenous to the Midwest part of the United States. Bill was a natural tour guide and loved explaining all the scientific facts about the fish. Fishing was one of his favorite recreational activities. He considered himself an expert fly fisherman. He bragged to Phyllis about all the trout he had caught. Michigan had a wide variety of trout and other fish. Phyllis listened to these facts intently, interjecting her opinions constantly.

Next they visited the Dossin Great Lakes Museum. This museum was credited with having the world's largest collection of scale-model Great Lakes ships and maritime memorabilia. It had a lot of "special hands-on exhibits."

After the museum tour, they went to the Anna Scripps Whitcomb Conservatory. This beautiful building was patterned after Thomas Jefferson's Monticello. It had permanent displays of ferns, palms, and one of the largest collections of orchids in the United States. A favorite was an exhibit that had samples of all the hundreds of different types of vegetation in the Detroit area. Phyllis and Bill spent a long time looking at these. They also admired the architecture of the building. Phyllis would love this type of early American architecture her entire life.

Next they went to the children's zoo. This was built to enable children to look at and literally play with some of the animals. Phyllis used to love this when she was younger. It had been a favorite of all the Arquette children. The zoo was built on thirteen acres and was encircled by a safari adventure with an elevated walkway for viewing. It had over 160 animals in a simulated but close-to-natural environment. It was a precursor for the modern zoos of the future.

Their Belle Isle date ended at the Scott Memorial Fountain. An eccentric gambler named James Scott bequeathed his entire fortune to build this huge, carved, white marble fountain. It used multicolored light art shows that started at dusk and lasted until the park closed. They enjoyed these for a half hour and then sadly returned to the ferry. They both enjoyed this tranquil place, which allowed a person to escape the realities of the Depression. Mostly silent, they held hands the entire way home.

While they were on the streetcar, Phyllis asked Bill, "What are your goals? Do you want to stay at Plymouth? Do you like being an engineer?"

"Well, I am not sure that Plymouth is the perfect match for me. I have always wanted to work at Ford. But I have a great job and the money is terrific, especially considering Detroit's economic situation. I love being an engineer and love the automotive business. There are so many opportunities. I want to get married, build a nice house, and have a family. What about you?" Bill answered.

"I would have loved finishing college. It was so perfect for me. But things don't always work out. I love my father, but I will never forget what he did. I have gotten over it and still visit him. Also, I have to check on Johnny and Bobbie. I like my job but can't see a lifetime doing it. I think I would love to have a family. Do you think there is a war coming? Do you think the Depression will ever end?" Phyllis asked.

"War might be inevitable. I know Plymouth is already making plans in the event they have to retool and make military goods. The Depression will end, but it looks like it has a few more years to run. There is still not a lot of demand for automobiles at this time. The New Deal programs helped some, but it doesn't seem like it is the right way to do things. We need to help businesses more. The wealth creators are in the private sector. I loved the Civilian Conservation Corps that I participated in during one summer, and it did a lot. It helped a large number of young men who needed money to help their families, and it helped our environment. The private sector has to get going again. Anyway, enough philosophy. I really like you and think we could have something special together." Bill got the nerve to make this last statement. It made Phyllis smile with happiness.

On the streetcar going home, Bill told Phyllis that he was going to buy a new car. He said that his salary was enough to afford this and that he had to look like a proper future executive.

"Let's go to Bob-Lo next Sunday. I will pick you up around nine. We can spend the whole day together," Bill said.

"Of course, love to go. That would be so much fun. I will be ready around nine in the morning and I will bring my dancing shoes." She smiled as she said this.

"It's a date then, and I will bring my dancing shoes too," Bill quipped.

Chapter 23

Bill arrived early Sunday morning at Phyllis's apartment. He was driving his brand-new black Plymouth. It sparkled in the sun, as Bill had already waxed and shined it. He was extremely proud of his first car. His dark Irish hair seemed darker now. His wireless glasses and mustache would be his trademark for years to come. He looked every bit like the new executive/engineer.

Phyllis dressed up more than usual. Her hair was turning browner but still had its curls. She was wearing bright red lipstick with light blue eye shadow, but with no other makeup. For years to come, she would rarely leave the house without her lipstick and eye shadow. She wore large dangling earrings. This became one of her trademarks. When her blonde hair darkened in later years, she would dye her hair bright red. This became another of her trademarks. Bill opened the door for her and they slowly made their way to the dock at the foot of Woodward Avenue. He drove slowly so that people could admire his new car.

They took the steamship *Columbia*. On the way they talked about their families. Phyllis started by asking Bill how his family was doing.

"Actually, things are going good now. My father has returned from his long hiatus and is no longer drinking. He wears the guilt on his face, but is relieved he has finally conquered this horrible disease. He has returned to work. He will never have the power or position he used to have, but, thanks to God, he is all right. Mom is doing well and is very happy—the happiest she has been since I was very little. I can tell she is proud of me and proud of herself for all the self-sacrifice. My sister is doing well. Her husband is doing well as an electrician. They have three children. My parents have bought a new house. How is your family doing, Phyll?"

"We are all doing well. All the Arquette children have moved out of the house now. The seven Arquette kids have grown up to be strong. My father and stepmother have bought a farm out in Saline. It had been foreclosed because of the Depression, so they got it for practically nothing. It is a working farm. All my older brothers are working and married. My sisters are married and their husbands have jobs. Somehow the Arquette family has survived the Depression. We are blessed."

They arrived at Bob-Lo and went directly to the dance pavilion. Its size and brilliance were overwhelming. The band would start at 2:00 PM, so they had time to walk around the small island. The island still had its natural beauty. They held hands and said little. Phyllis's dancing shoes had heels, making up for some of the height difference. Their first kiss was on this walk. Their hearts were forever linked.

They returned to the pavilion just as the band was starting. They danced for almost two hours, only taking breaks for food and a Faygo red pop. Faygo pop was another Detroit icon. Its ads would become part of every Detroiter's memories. "Which way did he go? Which way did he go? He went for Faygo," was their famous slogan. It was echoed by a small cowboy with a big hat. This ad would run in Detroit for years to come.

The trip home on the *Columbia* was tranquil and quiet. They had never had such a romantic day. They got off the ship at Woodward and Bill proudly took Phyllis home in the sparkling new Plymouth. They kissed again as they said "goodbye." This time they didn't have to even mention about meeting the next Sunday. It was now part of their routine and the most important day of their lives. Butterflies filled their stomachs and they ached as they separated.

Bill and Phyllis had many more fantastic dates in 1940. This was the time of big dance halls and big bands. The city was starting to vibrate with the "swing" music. Detroit had many fantastic ballrooms. The most famous were the Graystone Ballroom, the Walled Lake Casino, Edgewater Park, the Jefferson Beach Pavilion, the Grande Ballroom, and the Vanity Ballroom. Golden bands of swing featuring Glenn Miller, Glen Gray, Artie Shaw, Russ Morgan, Ozzie Nelson with his wife Harriet Hilliard, Hal Kemp, Benny Goodman, Skinner Ennis, Guy Lombardo, and Harry James would play at the beautiful ballrooms of Detroit. Famous singers like Perry Como, Danny Thomas, Louis Armstrong, and Betty Hutton, and local singers like Johnny Desmond and Janet Blair would sing at these ballrooms. The people utilized this entertainment and dancing to escape the pangs of the still-bad economic times.

Saturday nights were reserved for going out to dance, but Sundays were reserved for their favorite place in Detroit: Belle Isle. They would sometimes reserve one of the canoes. The canoes at Belle Isle were well known. They were elaborately decorated with two large seats and a Victrola. One of the canals at the island was described affectionately as Detroit's "love canal." The sounds of music filled the island.

On one of these trips Bill brought up the idea of marriage.

"Phyll, I think we are meant to be," he said. "What do you think?"

"Bill, I have felt this way since the eighth grade. I dreamed about us being together, but felt it was just that—a dream. I thought you would end up with Natalie like your mother wanted; and what about the rumors about you and the teacher who wrote in your yearbook, 'Bill, just the right size'? What about that?" Phyllis had always wanted to ask him this.

"Honest, Phyll, I don't know what she meant by that. I never knew you saw that." Bill was clearly embarrassed.

"Well, you asked me to sign your yearbook and I saw it."

"We would make a wonderful pair. I don't care about other girls. I only care about you." Bill quickly changed the subject.

"Billie (she never called him this), are you asking me to marry you?"

"I am not sure yet, but I have been thinking about it a lot."

"Well, don't wait too long. There are lots of beaus out there who 'might be the right size.'" She couldn't resist the chance to kid him.

Bill smiled and resumed the rowing. He just wasn't ready to make the big decision. They slowly paddled down the canal and listened to the music.

They continued their dating into the spring of 1941. With war clouds everywhere it was hard to make plans. Japan was expanding in Asia and the Pacific Ocean, and Germany was taking over most of Europe. Detroit plants were retooling and making plans to built military vehicles and parts. Bill was placed on a committee to determine how long it would take to retool. He had already gained a good reputation at Plymouth and was touted for higher management.

On a beautiful spring day in April 1941, Phyllis and Bill again went to their favorite place on earth. The flowers were blooming on the island. They went for a walk on one of the beautiful nature trails. They reached a place next to a small waterfall. The sound of flowing water was tranquilizing. They sat on a small bench facing the waterfall. They both had butterflies flying in their stomachs. Bill reached out to hold Phyllis's hand.

"Phyll, I completely love you. I know you like no other person in the world. I love being with you and need you to make me whole." He took out a small box, opened it, and asked Phyllis if she would accept his ring and marry him.

Starting to cry, Phyllis quickly replied, "Of course. Of course I will. I love you also." The dream that this day would come started at Belle Isle when a brash boy tried to cut in line. And the first day at Mackenzie rekindled this dream. She always remembered entering the school and hearing students greeting a boy as he walked down the hallway. "Hey, O'Slattery, what's new? Hey, Bill, how's it going?" And a boy with a deep, confident voice would answer back to each student. She would retell this story many times.

They didn't take long to get married. They had a small but eloquent wedding on Flag Day, June 14, 1941. Kit Karson was best man and his new wife, Doris (the former Doris Krause), was the matron of honor. Brianne, daughter of sister Tulah, was the flower girl. Phyllis and Bill looked extremely happy in their wedding photo. Their difference in size was still pronounced, but somehow it seemed to be just right. It was a marriage of two incredibly gifted people, who both became successful despite their difficult childhoods. Their wedding picture had a glow to it as if heaven was shining down on them.

Part II

Chapter 24

"We've had to put in a requisition for six people to replace you."

ill and Phyllis O'Slattery designed and built a house on Freeland Street in Detroit and moved in before the end of 1941. Bill's engineering skills were beneficial, but he essentially listened to his new wife regarding how the house should be designed.

Bill continued his work with Chrysler-Plymouth. His first job had been as a plant layout engineer, which he held for three years. He was promoted to assistant plant engineer and held this job until he left in 1947. He obtained valuable experience in the construction and organization of plants, which he was able to use a few years later at the Ford Motor Company. During World War II, he was involved in the defense industry. Products produced in his plant were tank parts, airplane parts for wings and landing gears, and antiaircraft guns (machining and assembly).

He had become dissatisfied with Chrysler-Plymouth and decided to venture out into other areas. He obtained a job in August 1947 at Akron, Ohio, as chief engineer for the Robinson Clay Product Company.

During that time period, Bill and Phyllis had three children. Their oldest son, Mark, was born in 1942, son Raymond was born in 1944, and Nancee was born in 1947. They moved to Akron with two young boys and a baby girl. It would not be easy for Phyllis to live in Akron; in fact, she was miserable. She missed the support of her family. The seven Arquette siblings were very close and loved to gather at reunions, first communions, confirmations, and other family events.

Phyllis was extremely homesick and told Bill she needed to return to Detroit. One day she said that she was "taking the family back to Detroit with or without" him. She was that unhappy.

Without giving it a thought, Bill agreed to immediately look for another job in Detroit. With his impressive resume and job skills, he was immediately able to acquire a position with the Ford Motor Company. His first job was as the supervisor of a production management department in the Rouge area manufacturing plants. He supervised ten process engineers.

He started with a group of young engineers who immensely respected and liked each other. This group bonded and they all promised they would help each other as they went up the ladder of success. One of these, John McHale, and his wife were family friends the rest of their lives.

In January 1949, the O'Slattery family returned to Detroit. They bought a house on Beaverland on the west side of Detroit. The days living on Beaverland would be wonderful for the O'Slattery family.

Bill quickly rose up the corporate ladder. He became an expert on facilities development and management. In 1955 he was one of a very few who were put in charge of developing a new Lincoln division within the Ford Motor Company. Part of this job included the design and development of a new assembly plant for Lincolns at Wixom, Michigan. This was about an hour from downtown Detroit.

Because of the long drive each day, the O'Slatterys moved in May 1957 to Northville, Michigan. This was only a few miles from Wixom.

Bill and Phyllis would live in Northville the rest of their lives, except for a three-year period during which Bill was assigned to Ford of Europe. They became leaders in this community. Phyllis loved Northville and would thrive there. Some called her "Miss Northville."

Bill worked at Wixom for a few years and then was promoted to a position in Dearborn, Michigan. He worked in various management positions in Dearborn until the early 1970s, when he was asked by John McHale to work with him for Ford of Europe. He was near the end of his career and felt this would be a great way to end it. Phyllis was extremely excited about the opportunity to travel throughout Europe. They decided to take the job.

Bill and Phyllis returned to Northville in 1976, at which time Bill decided to retire. On January 20, 1977, there was a retirement dinner for Bill in Southfield, Michigan. After a lot of good-natured kidding, the master of ceremonies finished his talk by saying, "Bill, seriously, we want to express our thanks to you for twenty-seven years of dedicated and distinguished service. We've jibbed and jabbed at you, Bill, but it was meant in good fun. We congratulate you and also congratulate your lovely wife, Phyllis. We all know that it takes a wonderful marriage and partner to get through the difficult tasks we have to undertake. You might like to know that we've put in a requisition for six people to replace you. That's the first impact of how much we are going to miss you. Good luck and best wishes from all your associates and friends in the Ford Motor Company—everywhere!"

Chapter 25

In June of 1979 I received a call from my sister, Nancee. She told me my father had suffered a heart attack and was taken to the hospital. Without packing I got in my car and drove to the airport. When I arrived at the Detroit Metro Airport, I was met by my father-in-law. The look on his face told me what I didn't want to know, but I still asked him about my father.

"He didn't make it," he sadly said.

My legs buckled and I felt like I was going to fall over. I couldn't believe it. My father was only sixty-three years old. He had just retired and was really enjoying his new life. His daily routine was to read the paper and drink coffee, work on the family tree, and then go to the golf course if the weather permitted. One of the things he absolutely loved to do was play golf. With his work schedule and the Michigan weather, he had a very difficult time pursuing this hobby. I remember how sad he would be when he had taken a Saturday off to play golf and it rained or was too cold.

One of the saddest things I have ever done was to clean out his locker at the local golf course. He was unique and his own man, and he didn't worry about convention and what others did. He loved the color green and had sweaters, shirts, and even socks of various shades of green. He loved to wear a fisherman's type hat with a clear visor rather than a traditional golf hat. He only ordered Titleist golf balls with the number seven on them. That way, he would never forget the number of his golf ball if he had to identify it in the rough. He loved Clark candy bars and had at least several dozen packages. He also liked the type of golf sweaters that were without sleeves, and he had several of these also—all green. I could hardly hold back the tears when I was doing this. His many golfer friends stopped by and offered their condolences.

My mother was holding up well but needed some help. I helped her pick out the casket and the tombstone and went to the funeral home to make arrangements. I also called the relatives and friends. Hundreds of people showed up for the viewing. Keeping busy made it slightly easier to get through the worst time of my life. I also met with a friend who was a minister. Northville was a small town and everyone knew personally the important people in town. Even though my father was a Catholic, my mother wanted Northville's popular minister to give the eulogy. My father made sure all his children were brought up Catholic; however, my mother went along with this reluctantly. She went to mass on Sunday but never converted to the Catholic faith.

The funeral was held at the Catholic church in Northville. The church was totally full. Representatives from the Ford Motor Company came, including its president. Family, friends, and relatives all came. I was able to hold off my tears until the eulogy was given.

The "wake" was held at my mother's house. When it was over, my sister, Nancee, and I went out to the backyard and talked. We talked about the things we remembered about growing up.

Neither of us could remember very much about the house on Freeland Street. Nancee was a newborn and I was very young. One vivid recollection was when my brother and I received bicycles for Christmas. My brother's bicycle had a very large front wheel. He always would say how much he hated that bicycle because it made him feel self-conscious.

Living in Akron was also a vague memory. Again, I had one vivid memory. We had a squirrel living in a tree on our front lawn. The squirrel became very violent and actually bit my father. The police came out to kill it and one of the policemen was also bitten. Finally, the squirrel was killed with a belly club. It was tested for rabies and, fortunately, the tests were negative. There was an article with a cartoon caricature of the squirrel on the front page of the Akron newspaper.

We both agreed we loved living on Beaverland Street when we returned to Detroit. It was sort of a "Mackenzie" for us. We had dozens of friends and always something to do. We could walk to the nearest grade school and run home for lunch to watch Soupy Sales on TV.

Nancee said the following: "I loved playing house with all the girls on the street. We each had a playhouse with furniture and other household goods. Girls rarely played sports, but we all loved playing with our newest doll."

I remembered all the ball games we played in the street. We played baseball every chance we got. It taught us to hit up the middle. Manhole covers, drains, and patches of tar served as the bases. We also played touch football on the street. We played tackle football in nearby Rouge Park. When it got colder, we played hockey on the ponds in this beautiful park. I also remember lots and lots of games of hide-and-seek, army games with Korean War surplus equipment, and "cowboys and Indians." Riding our bikes all over the place was a constant activity. We rode our bikes to the grocery store on Plymouth Road and bought candy, pop, and sports cards. I wish I still had all those Mickey Mantle rookie cards. We traded the cards and sometimes used them on our bikes to make noise. We used clothespins to attach the cards to the spokes. They make a fantastic noise. We made up games to play without any of the fancy equipment of today. I remember that a punishment was to have to come inside. We were allowed to play until dark and were expected to immediately return home. Few violated this rule, because of a fear of not being able to go outside the next day.

Nancee continued, "We girls loved to play hopscotch on the

sidewalks and alleyways. We drew the lines with chalk. We also loved to play the game called 'jacks.' Remember that one?" (I nodded yes)

"We all enjoyed going to Brennan Pools, which we could ride our bikes to. Television was still a novelty and watching a TV show was a family event. Families had one TV set, and they would gather around it to watch. TV shows like *The Ed Sullivan Show*, *The Milton Berle Show*, *Ozzie and Harriet*, *I Love Lucy*, and *The Carol Burnett Show* brought families together. Today, it seems that TV separates families, as many houses have a TV in every room. I remember Dad always asking, 'When is Gleason on?' He could never remember the day or time. He loved watching Jackie Gleason."

We both agreed that there was a very strict division of labor in our house. We were a very typical middle-class family. The father went to work and brought home the paycheck. The mother ran the household. Mother did all the cooking, cleaning, bill paying, and child rearing. The father was expected to carry out punishments when he got home and to be a role model. Fortunately, our father was not into corporal punishment or anything like that. It was usually a severe lecture and reprimand. We both agreed on how wonderful our family life was and how much we respected both parents.

Nancy reminisced: "I think some of my favorite memories were our vacations to Traverse City, Michigan. We always stayed at Baker's Acres, which had cabins on the shoreline of Grand Traverse Bay. We used to go for two or three weeks every summer. Dad had to sometimes take us there and return to work for a week or so. I remember all the fantastic friends we had. The same families would schedule their vacations for the same time in the summer. Traverse City was a fantastic place. The yearly cherry parade was attended by all. I remember the Native American who rode his palomino horse at the end of each parade. People in the parade would throw cherries to the spectators. The people of Traverse City call it the Cherry Capital of the World."

I interjected, "I remember our trips to Bob-Lo. Those ferryboats were so fun and the amusement park was fantastic. We went with our cousins. We all loved the ride called the Caterpillar, which enclosed its riders as it rode around in a circle. Dodgem Cars were my most favorite thing. We would get into these small cars and smash into each other."

"Christmastime was my favorite," continued Nancee. "Mom and Dad did not spoil us throughout the year, but they did at Christmas. Mom really loved Christmas. Trimming the family tree was so much fun. I always got a new doll each Christmas and it began my doll collection. I collected dolls throughout all my younger years. I also loved our Sunday dinners. It was the one time Dad ate with us on a regular basis. He usually would leave for work before we ate our breakfast and return home after we had eaten. Mom always saved a plate for him. Sunday dinners were so fun because we would talk and talk about our lives. I remember Dad saying he was a boss, so he wanted to set an example. He wanted to be the first person at the office and the last one to leave."

I continued, "The one activity Dad was able to fit into his busy schedule was the Cub Scouts. Many of the fathers living on Beaverland Street got involved, and they had more fun than the kids. The other thing we regularly did was go to the Detroit Lions games. In the 1950s the Lions were a powerhouse, as they won three championships. We went to the 1957 championship game. It was great. The Lions beat their rivals the Cleveland Browns 59–14, avenging a 56–10 loss in the 1954 championship game. Dad and the boys went to the noon Thanksgiving game and you stayed with Mom and cooked the dinner. Talk about a change from today's world. Mom got us into golf when she took advantage of free lessons for kids at the nearby River Rouge Golf Course."

"Do you remember moving to Northville in 1957?" I asked. (Nancy nodded her head.) "It was one of the worst days of my life. We went from a city block with houses almost touching to a rural subdivision. There were only about ten houses in the entire subdivision. Today there are over a hundred. I remember the sounds of crickets and hated them, as I had a difficult time sleeping. Dad was helping to build the Wixom plant and he needed to get closer to work."

Nancy said, "All in all, growing up in Northville was a good experience. The schools were good and we were all able to participate in tons of activities. Eventually we adjusted and made new friends. We still went to Traverse City, Bob-Lo, and amusement parks like Edgewater Park. I liked my time at Northville High School."

I nodded my head in agreement and continued, "In Northville Mark and I were in charge of yard work. He cut the back lawn and I cut the front lawn. We were expected to do the weeding and other yard work. One thing we did with Dad was to go into the woods and get small shrubs and trees. Mark and I planted dozens of trees. They are huge now and you can barely see the house. Dad totally designed the house. He had bad knees from his football days and didn't want any stairs, so it was one story. It was an extremely roomy and practical house. It was made totally of red brick. However, Mom never liked it. She loved the early American era and always wanted a colonial-style house. I remember her making Dad put some pillars in the front to make it a little less plain. He and Mark did the labor themselves. It was all red brick. Personally, I liked it. We each had our own bedroom. Mark and I had shared a bedroom in the Beaverland home."

"Do you remember when Dad was up for promotion? The Ford Motor Company would send out people to size up his family life. A 'suitable' wife and well-behaved children were part of an evaluation for promotion. This started during the Henry Ford days when he was trying to promote the entire family being involved with the job. Mom was able to charm them each time. She was good at that. We were expected to dress up and to not speak unless we were spoken to. 'Children are to be seen, not heard' was the attitude. I guess we passed the test."

I also remember all the fun times we had with the Arquette family. We usually got together at Doris's house. We played baseball, horseshoes, and lots of other games. Uncle Buster was really into horseshoes. The men would get together and play pinochle and drink Goebel's and Stroh's beer, both Detroit beers. The women would spend hours preparing fantastic meals.

We both talked about how much we respected our father. He truly was a role model. We also talked about how unfair it was that he died at such an early age. He got robbed of his well-deserved long retirement. "The automobile business had worn him out." We both agreed.

Our mother walked out to the patio where Nancee and I had been reminiscing. Her eyes were red and she looked so sad. We had never seen her look like that before.

"Are you going to be okay, Mom?" we asked.

"Call us anytime you need us."

"I just have to keep moving. I still have my family and my club work in Northville. I will just have to keep moving," she said, holding back the tears.

Chapter 26

"I will never hear Nancee's sweet little voice again."

A little over two years after my father passed away, I got another one of those calls that no one wants to get. My brother called me and told me about my sister being in an automobile accident. I knew what was coming as he told me she did not survive the crash. He reassured me that Matt and Dan were all right. She had been out in the countryside near Grand Rapids volunteering to help at a convent. Her thoughts must have been elsewhere when she ran a stop sign and was hit on the driver's side. Apparently she was not wearing a seat belt. The thoughts that came to my mind were of disbelief. *I must be dreaming.* My initial feelings were of anger. *How could this be allowed to happen?* That anger still stays with me. Again I made the dreadful trip to Michigan.

Nancee was a gifted writer. She wrote the most beautiful letters. The words flowed from her pen. She published numerous articles as a freelance writer. She was in the process of writing a historical fiction novel set in the Revolutionary War times.

There was one event I will never forget. She was in a class in high school when the news came that President John Kennedy had been shot. She loved John Kennedy. She was so distraught that she had to go to the nurse's office, and she stayed there the entire day.

My mother was devastated. One thing she said still stays with me: "I will never hear Nancee's sweet little voice again." Nancee was a sweet, lovely, talented young lady. She worshiped her two sons, had developed a new interest in helping animals, was active in her church, and was involved in many charities. She was only thirty-three years old. Her son Dan was eight and her son Matt was eleven at the time. They were both in the car, but miraculously they were not injured.

My mother knew she had to help her two grandsons. For the better part of the next decade, she was again thrust into the role of surrogate mother.

The following was written by her grandson Matthew. It anecdotally describes a lot about my mother, their relationship, and how my mother helped them.

> One of the defining moments of my adolescence occurred in a local Sears's store. My Grandmother had taken me shopping for school clothes one late summer afternoon, as she did many times after coming to take care of my brother and me after our Mother—my Grandmother's only daughter—died in a car accident. On the way to the mall I was teasing her. My brother and I would often tease her and she would give it right back. Today, I was as usual teasing her about her slow driving and how she couldn't even see over the steering wheel of the boat of a car she drove. She would take the teasing in stride but with a great sense of humor would usually threaten a "knuckle sandwich" if I didn't pipe down. When we were finally in the store, my Grandma, always all business, found a clerk and asked where the "husky" sizes could be found for her grandson. This was in the 1980s and was before "husky" was a more common name for an actual size. The clerk happened to be a an attractive young woman; and, I, a chubby

awkward teen (I'd added puberty pounds, as some boys do, and had gained a few pounds from feasting regularly on the delicious burgers that my Grandmother was known for) couldn't have been more embarrassed. Yet, looking back, I realized my Grandmother was being kind when she used the word "husky." She was being very tactful, a skill she had in "spades," among so many other skills.

That evening at home she grilled up some of her famous burgers for my younger brother and me with a side of chips and a bottle of root beer. Later, we watched George Kell and Al Kaline, ex-Tiger stars; call the Tigers game on TV. By the seventh inning we were mixed up in a game of Monopoly and guffawing again about Kaline's predictable disappearance for a few innings. "He's off for a hot dog!" she'd say, a little giddily after having taken a wee sip of bubbly that night, as she occasionally did.

We had many of those nights, together, as much a family as we could have hoped for, all things considered. My Grandmother was a remarkable woman, and I miss her dearly. I am glad to shop for my own pants these days, though, a thought that I think would make her chuckle.

While helping to raise her "third family," she was becoming more and more involved with the clubs of Northville and in organizing a town hall series for the town. Eventually she narrowed her time to the Northville Garden Club. One of her busiest tasks was to write and edit their monthly newsletter. She did this mostly in Grand Rapids. The newsletters were quite professional in their size and quality. They were filled with "Phyllis witticisms."

She was also finding time to share with her other two children and the grandchildren from their marriages.

I also asked Daniel to write down some of his memories of the times spent with his grandmother during this time period. He wrote the following:

> Right after my mom's death, one of my most vivid memories I have of that time was of Grandma. She had lost her husband and only daughter within a very short time, both in tragic ways. The memory was at my Mother's wake, when there were many people at our house. I had walked upstairs and saw Grandma. She was walking very slowly, hunched over, much more than usual, taking the steps one-by-one, and even though I was only eight years old, I remember the deep sense of sadness, sorrow, and pain on her face, perhaps having aged many years in a very short period of time.
>
> She didn't start living with us at the house in Grand Rapids right away, but visited and helped out often. My other Grandparents had moved in. I think they were trying to help and it also served as a "halfway" point between the Upper Peninsula and their soon-to-be new home in Florida. Within a year, however, Grandma O'Slattery had actually decided to take over much of the raising of Matt and I, with my Father having returned to work and being very busy. She set up camp in what was previously my parents' room, which among other things, must have been extremely difficult for her, with the memory of my Mother and the echoes of her soft voice and laughter still reverberating through the house, her presence undoubtedly felt everywhere in the two little blonde haired kids, the grieving, widowed husband, the white terrier, and perhaps even finding long strands of her golden hair.

Grandma probably took solace in what in many ways turned out to be her raising Matt and I, maybe seeing her daughter in us, keeping the memory of Nancee alive; and toil she did—two active kids, each with our own challenges—she put mile after mile on her odometer, hauling us back and forth to baseball games, friends' houses, school, etc. She prepared breakfast, lunch and dinner every day. This went on for years. She travelled back and forth to Northville a weekend or two a month, often with Matt and me. It may have been a bittersweet departure for her, as she received a "break" from the stresses of three males in one household, but facing the inevitable solitude of loneliness that awaited her at her house in Northville with not only the memories of her lost daughter on her mind, but also her beloved husband William, his rim-bespectacled countenance, with the sly and confident Irish grin, keeping watch over her from the multiple photos strewn throughout the house.

Round three of raising children was possibly the most difficult for Grandma. In many ways she was an amazing woman, of course, and I'll never forget her kindness, generosity and biting wit. She stayed with us for most of the decade. The memories are, of course, fading into the past. Confusing and painful most of the time but also filled with laughter and comfort.

The experience of losing my Mother at an early age and being raised by my maternal Grandmother has had an enormous impact on all of our lives. I owe a lot to Grandma O'Slattery.

After a decade, Phyllis returned to her home in Northville. She still helped her grandchildren, but it was now time to move on. The loneliness of being at home must have been unbearable. But my mom was not an ordinary person. She was comfortable in a material sense, but she didn't want to sit at home and do nothing. She returned to her role as a leader. She would become one of the most important people in her new "Mackenzie"—Northville, Michigan.

Chapter 27

"If she were here with us today, she would
be telling everyone where to sit."

hyllis O'Slattery stayed mentally alert into her early eighties. Her work for the garden club had helped tremendously. In returning to her natural role, she often became an officer and usually the president of the clubs she joined. She was president of the garden club and the women's club. I am convinced that she should have been a governor. She never wanted to remarry. She would always say that no one could ever replace Bill O'Slattery.

She seemed to wear out by the end of the 1990s. In the summer of 1999, my family visited her in Northville. She was still functioning, but her short-term memory was not as good as it was. She had lost her driver's license and rarely got out of the house. Her brother and sister-in-law, who lived within ten miles, would buy her food, help out with the bills, and take her places. They did a great job.

However, I received another one of those dreaded calls in January of 2000. My uncle told me that my mom had gotten sick from the flu and was in really bad shape. I again had to rush to Michigan. I had a really bad feeling about what was happening. She had almost died and had lost almost all her memory. We knew she needed assisted living. I took a leave of absence from work and moved into her home. With help from others, we took care of what needed to be done. We found a great assisted-living place, and she recovered some in the next few years. Until the last year or so, she remembered who I was. I was living about five hundred miles away and was basically going back and forth every other weekend. She was well taken care of at this assisted-living facility for the next six years. I loved the staff. They were so helpful. One lady allowed me to call her on a regular basis and get progress reports.

One of the last things I remember her saying was, "I am feeling chipper today". That was one of her favorite expressions.

In August of 2006 I again received an awful call. This time it was from a hospital. My mother had become very ill and had been admitted to a hospital. I flew to Michigan and found her in a coma. I could tell her death was imminent. It was so sad. She held on for a few days and I was able to plan the funeral, burial, wake, and other things. I was in her room with the hospice people when her breathing became more difficult. A sweet hospice nun was there to help me. Her prayers were soothing. I was holding Mom's hand as she died.

I helped the priest write the eulogy for her mass. It had been the first time she had been in church since my sister had died. She said she never could forgive God for allowing her daughter to die so young. I always hoped she had worked this out somehow. If anyone should be in heaven, it is my mother. I asked the priest to give the eulogy, as I knew I could never get through it.

The most important thing he emphasized in the eulogy was how Phyllis had raised three families. Another thing was how she loved to be in control. He said, "If Phyllis was with us today, she would be telling everyone where to sit." Everyone laughed quietly, for they knew what he was talking about. He mentioned her children, grandchildren, and great-grandchildren.

My mother's story should be told. Her life was incredible. She is the strongest person I have ever known.

References

1. "How the Great Depression Changed Detroit," by Kenny Nolan, *The Detroit News.*
www.detnews.com/history/depress/depress.htm -- obtained June 2003.

2. "The Purple Gang, Purple Story," GeoCities.
www.geocities.com/jiggs2000_us/purple.html -- obtained June 2003

3. "Bootlegger's Paradise," Crime Library.
Gangsters & Outlaws/Unique Gang Organizations, The Purple Gang,
By Mark Gribben
www.crimelibrary.com/gangsters/purple/purplemain.htm -- obtained
June 2003

4. "The 1925 Chrysler Roadster," Hubcap Cafe.
www.hubcapcafe.com/ocs/pages01/chry2501.htm -- obtained June 2003

5. "King of the Ring," by Ed Dunn, *The Buffalonian*, News as History.
www.buffalonian.com/hnews/1945slattery.html -- obtained June 2003

6. "How J. L. Hudson Changed the Way We Shop," *The Detroit News,*
by Vivian M. Baulch, Special to The News.
www.detnews.com/history/hudon/hudson.htm -- Obtained June 2003

7. "Detroit's Historic Fox Theatre," by Laurie J. Marzejka, *The Detroit News*.
www.detnews.com/history/fox/fox.htm -- Obtained June 2003

8. "Bob-Lo, Island of White Wood," by Jenny Nolan, *The Detroit News*.
www.detnews.com/history/boblo.history.htm -- Obtained June 2003

9. "When Detroit Danced to the Big Bands," by Patricia Zacharias, *The Detroit News*.
www.detnews.com/history/dancing/ -- Obtained June 2003

10. National Park Service: Belle Isle
www.cr.nps.gov/nr/travel/detroiot/d6.htm -- Obtained June 2003

11. "John Miller's Big Dipper at Jefferson Beach."
www.home.nyc.rr.com/johnmiller/jefferson.html -- Obtained June 2003

12. "The Fox Theatre," Olympia Entertainment.
www.olympiaentertainment.com/Fox/home.asp -- Obtained June 2003

13. "Snack Foods and Pop, Detroit Style," by Vivian Baulch, *The Detroit News*.
www.detnews.com/history/vernors/vernors.htm -- Obtained June 2003

14. Various issues and articles from the *Mackenzie Dial,* the Mackenzie High School newspaper.

15. Article from the program at Mackenzie High School's Tenth Anniversary.